Seasons of Albadone

THE EIGHTH CHANT SERIES

ÉLAN MARCHÉ
CHRISTOPHER WARMAN

This is a work of fiction. Names, characters, places, and incidents either are the product of the author's imagination or are used fictitiously. Any resemblance to actual persons, living or dead, events, or locales is entirely coincidental.

Copyright © 2020 by Christopher Warman & Élan Marché

All rights reserved.

The moral rights of the author have been asserted.

Second paperback edition June 2022

Cover art by Tim Kelly
Map art by Dewi Hargreaves

ISBN 979-8-218-02552-6

Contents

PROLOGUE 1

AUTUMN: An Enchantress 4
    I.   The Woods of Albadone 5
    II.   The Cabin 16
    III. A Visitor 25
    IV. The Hunt 37
    V.   The Cost 48

WINTER: A Father 59
    VI.   A Drunk 60
    VII. A Wasted Workday 70
    VIII. The Wishing Tree 82
    IX.   The Tree's Gift 94

SPRING: A Foreman 106
    X.   Black Air 107
    XI.   Black Water 120
    XII. A Darkness So Dim 132
    XIII. A Light That Never Dies 144

SUMMER: A Mother 155
    XIV. Scars 156
    XV.   The Rat's Nest 168
    XVI. A Dark Escape 181
    XVII. To Sacrifice 192

PROLOGUE

THE STORY OF THE SEASONS

In the beginning of time, the True One created all that ever was: the lands, the waters that cut through them, the sky, and the trees that reached for it. The True One smiled and marveled at what He had made, for it was perfect.

One day, the *dragons* came to Him.

"Hello brave *dragons*, Guardians of the mountains," the True One said, expecting a polite reply.

"It's not warm enough," the disgruntled *dragons* complained. "How are we to keep our flames alive?"

The True One was taken aback. "I was sure the warmth was perfect. But if it isn't enough for you brave *dragons*, I shall split the year into two seasons: one much warmer than the other."

The *dragons* returned to their mountains, content.

Time passed, and the *griffons* came to the True One.

"Hello valiant *griffons*, Guardians of the skies," He said, once again expecting a polite greeting.

"It's not windy enough," the ungrateful *griffons* cried. "How are we to soar across lands far and wide?"

"Now, there's no mistaking that the winds were perfect," the True One explained. "But if it isn't windy enough for you valiant *griffons*, I shall split the year into a third season of high winds."

The *griffons* returned to their skies, content.

More time passed, and the *mers* came to the True One.

"Hello gentle *mers*, Guardians of the waters," the True One said, now unsure that He was *ever* going to receive a polite reply.

"There's not enough water," the thankless *mers* declared. "How are we to swim from sea to sea when there's so much land in our path?"

The True One sighed. "I thought the amount was perfect. But if there isn't enough water for you gentle *mers*, I shall split the year into a fourth season of snow, so that the land may be covered in water, at least for a time."

The *mers* returned to their waters, content.

The True One watched as the four seasons passed—as heat scorched crops, winds uprooted trees, and snow froze the bodies of those who couldn't find shelter. "I thought I had made the perfect world."

Then, one day, the *melk* came to the True One.

"Let me guess," the True One lamented, "you wish for a season all to yourself, like those other Guardians?"

"We do not," the *melk* replied.

"Oh?" the True One intoned. "And what is it that you want of me, dear *melk*?"

"We wish only to offer our thanks," the *melk* praised, "for You have created the lands we inhabit, the skies that brighten our days and nights, and the waters that nourish and cleanse us."

The True One smiled upon the *melk*. Swiftly, He waved a mighty hand across the land. A forest of tall trees sprouted where His shadow passed. "As a reward for your unwavering thankfulness, humble *melk,* I gift you a land of wonders. As long as you care for it, you shall want for nothing."

The *melk* bowed their heads and thanked the True One. "We will name this land *Albadone,* and we shall guard it until the end of time."

"Of that I have no doubt," the True One said.

AUTUMN:
AN ENCHANTRESS

I.

THE WOODS OF ALBADONE

Puffs of gray smoke emerging from the brown and orange trees and rising into the sparsely clouded sky marred the otherwise breathtaking view of the forest of Albadone. It was a particularly biting Autumn morning, so anyone who wasn't already busy at work was huddled in their small homes by the warmth of a fire. Adriel envied them. She had left her cabin in the face-numbing darkness of early morning to fetch this and that for one of Mother Olla's many enchantments. The old woman was always busy with something, it was hard to keep track of exactly what she was doing. Adriel didn't really mind the early morning treks, as they allowed her the opportunity to meet with the woodsfolk neighbors that lived near their small home and explore the thick woods. *Anything to get out of that decrepit old cabin,* she thought to herself.

Autumn wasn't her least favorite season—Winter took that prize—but it was far from being her favorite. When she was a child especially, she could feel the trees pulsing with life strongly in the Spring and a bit more lazily in the Summer. But that also meant she could feel them as they became dormant in Autumn and slept miserably in the Winter, longing for Spring. She always felt sorry for them, even now that she knew it was just part of the Cycle of Nature. Mother Olla had told her that it was a good thing that she could feel the Cycle through the trees and that it was a sign that she would grow to become a powerful enchantress.

"One day," the old woman had told her during one of her lessons, "when you are whole, you will sense the Cycle of Nature not only in the trees but in everything that surrounds you: the soil, the wind, even the air you breathe." Adriel wasn't sure that was something she wanted. Hearing the fluctuating pain of the trees as they were forced asleep by the invisible hand of the Cycle had been at best a discomfort, at worse overwhelming. But Mother Olla had told her that sensing the Cycle was an important part of being an enchantress, and that was what Adriel wanted more than anything in the whole world.

The top of Chanter's Hill, where she now stood, held one of her favorite sights. The woods stretched out as far as the eye could see. The Womb of the World—the large black mountain where *life energy* itself was said to have originated at the beginning of time—was a ghostly apparition through the morning mist in the west, and barely visible, north of the mountain, was the High Tower of Vizen, where the royals were, no doubt, still asleep. Lately, a new structure had appeared in the landscape: in the center of the woods, a few miles south, a large wooden tower erupted from the trees like the arm of a drowning man from a mud-brown lake. Those folk had been hard at work building the tall structure for several weeks now. Mother Olla had scoffed and cursed, accusing the workers of corrupting the land—Adriel was almost sure Mother Olla had no idea what the thing was even supposed to be.

The girl removed her brown leather gloves and rubbed her stiff hands together. The sun had been out for the good part of an hour, but it would take several more before the air would warm. Her hood was pulled up, casting a sharp shadow over her eyes. Underneath, her ears were still struggling to thaw. Adriel put her gloves back on and turned towards the sparse gnarled trees growing atop the hill. The rotting corpse of a downed tree lay across the bulging roots of another. Adriel crouched in front of the hollow trunk and peeked inside: dark brown mushrooms covered in small holes lined the top of the trunk. They were called *poxcheek* mushrooms, as their lumpy texture resembled that of a pox-scarred face. The sickly-sweet smell of decay and moisture was an indication that they were ripe for harvest.

 Adriel unsheathed a small dagger—the one that was given to her by Mother Olla on her tenth year under the woman's tutelage—from her belt and began scraping the mushrooms into a small sack pouch until it was full. With a piece of twine, she closed the pouch and placed it gently inside her satchel. She scraped one last mushroom and placed it in her mouth. Its texture was soft and silky, melting in her mouth with each bite. The taste was not as pleasant, dirt at the forefront of the flavor, with a strange sweetness at the back end that reminded her of rotten nuts. It wasn't a flavor she loved, but she truly did enjoy the texture enough for her to forgive it. Adriel returned the knife to her belt and stood to her feet.

 She looked out to the forest one final time, filling her lungs with the cold Autumn air. When she exhaled, a cloud surrounded her and immediately vanished. She was making her way back to the beaten path that led down the hill when a sudden flash of silver light filled her vision and was gone in an instant. Adriel looked around the hilltop for what might have caused such a beam. From the angle, she assumed it must have been the sun reflecting off something on the ground. As she moved, her eyes caught another stab of blinding light. Now sure of the light's origin, Adriel approached a thorny bush. She carefully held the prickly branches aside and reached into the bush with her other hand. She felt a trail of white heat as a thorn scraped her arm, thankfully not enough to draw blood. She grabbed the mysterious object and slowly pulled her arm back out. In her hand was a silver feather, pointed at the end like a dagger and more reflective than a shard of glass when the sun caught it just right. When the sun wasn't on it, its vane refracted the light like a rainbow.

She had only ever seen something like it in one of Mother Olla's books. Most of those old tomes contained lists of ingredients and recipes for all sorts of enchantments, very few of them accompanied by illustrations. The full-paged image of a silver feather had always stood out to her, especially since it belonged to a creature called a *melk*, which the book classified as extinct. She twirled the feather between her gloved hands—sunlight bouncing crazily in every direction—and then placed it gingerly in her satchel.

Adriel made her way down the path. Browning leaves sloshed under her boots. The skeletal trunks of soon-to-be barren trees rose around her on either side like a ribcage as she descended, and a few moments later she reached the flat terrain below—the belly of the forest. A bead of sweat ran down her forehead after the demanding downhill walk despite the morning chill. From her satchel she produced a small leather flask and raised it to her lips, gulping the cold water much too quickly and causing a headache to rear up the back of her head to the bottom of her throat. Her brow furrowed with regret.

Children's voices trickled through the trees in the distance, followed by the approaching pitter-patter of tiny feet. A small smile appeared on Adriel's face. The girl bit her lip deviously and set her satchel at the base of a nearby tree. Slowly, she sneaked towards the origin of the voices, careful to neither make a sound nor be seen. As she moved closer, the voices became clear.

"You always get to decide what we play!" protested a young boy—Adriel was sure that was Hammen.

"I don't make the rules," explained another boy—Toller—"I am the eldest, so I always get to decide. We're playing builders!"

"But I want to play dragon hunters," whined Hammen.

"Quiet, you! I am your foreman," Toller said while putting on a deep voice. "We must build a tower to the sky so that—put that down Hammen!"

"A dragon hunter never lays down his sword!" Hammen proclaimed in his most heroic voice. Adriel suppressed a laugh.

"We're not playing *fucking* dragon hunters!" Toller yelled. A silence so deep filled the air that you could hear nearby leaves hit the ground.

"You said a bad word," Hammen accused. "I'm telling mother!" Adriel covered her mouth; it was becoming increasingly difficult to smother her laughter. She peeked around the tree in time to catch Hammen running off into the woods, pursued closely by his protesting older brother. It was now or never. Adriel ran out of her cover and chased down the two boys. She caught up to them quickly and snatched them into her arms—first Toller then Hammen—while making guttural screeches, her best impression of a dragon. Toller yelped as soon as his feet left the ground, while Hammen flailed about screaming "Let me go, let me go!"

"Never!" Adriel replied in a monstrous voice. "Once a dragon has its prey it never lets it go!"

"We're not playing dragon hunters!" Toller lamented.

Adriel dropped the boys on the ground and stopped to catch her breath. "My, you two are getting heavy." The girl made her way back to the tree where she had left the satchel, the two boys at her heel.

"What are you doing in the woods, Mother Adriel?" Toller asked, no doubt trying to distract his brother from the curse word he had said moments earlier. He had the same dark black hair as their father, but it was curly and untamed like their mother's. Hammen, on the other hand, was an anomaly, with his bright and fiery strawberry hair. Two things marked them as brothers: their green-gray eyes and their round cheeks, both of which they took after their mother, Yolta.

"I'm collecting some ingredients for Mother Olla," she explained. "She's working on an enchantment."

"I bet it's a flying potion!" Hammen exclaimed in that excited manner he always had.

Toller shook his head and spat. "There's no such thing as a flying potion."

"There is too!" Hammen explained frantically. "Like in the story!"

"Stories aren't real."

"Are too!"

"Are not!"

The argument continued back and forth like this until Adriel interrupted. "Do you want to see something special?" Adriel hoped she could make the boys stop arguing. They were dear children, but she didn't know how Yolta did it sometimes in a house full of men. Before the boys could answer, Adriel produced the *melk* feather from the satchel with a flourish. Hammen let out an elongated gasp, while Toller went wide-eyed in awe.

"Can I touch it?" was all Toller asked.

"Me too," Hammen was quick to add.

"One at a time," Adriel said while handing the feather to Toller. "And be gentle."

Toller twirled the feather between his fingers, sending silver rays of light bouncing across his face. "What is it?"

"I believe it's a *melk* feather," Adriel explained.

"Milk feather?" Hammen asked.

"She said *melk*, you dolt."

"Toller, be nice to your brother," Adriel admonished. She nodded towards the feather and then at Hammen. Toller sighed and handed the feather to his brother. The younger boy's eyes grew wide as he watched the rainbow crawl across the blade-like length of the feather. "What's a *melk*?" he asked.

"It's a very old creature, one that hasn't existed in these woods for many, many years. I plan on giving it to Mother Olla to see if, perhaps, she can make something from it."

"Can she make a flying potion with it?" Hammen asked excitedly. Toller rolled his eyes and groaned.

Adriel smiled and took the feather from Toller's hand. "Unfortunately, *melk* weren't flying creatures, but if I hear of a way to make a flying potion, you'll be the first one I tell." Hammen gave her a grin, exposing a hole in the top right side of his mouth where a baby tooth had recently fallen out.

"Are my boys giving you gripe?" Yolta appeared from nearby trees and joined the three. The young woman's heavy hooded cloak was untied and gently draped around her shoulders so that a wrap could be tied diagonally across her chest. In the wrap, her newborn boy Elger softly snoozed. Her hood was down, revealing thick auburn locks that freely cascaded across her shoulders. On her left arm was a basket full of glittering black berries. Her gray-green eyes—like her sons'—were immediately drawn to the silver feather in Adriel's hand.

"Not at all," Adriel said with a smile.

"You don't have to be polite. I know how these two are." Hammen ran to his mother and hugged her leg tightly, making the woman waver at the added weight.

Adriel turned to Toller and pointed at the basket. "Seems like your mother needs help with that." Toller groaned and begrudgingly took the basket from his mother. "Good boy."

Yolta nodded thankfully. "Say goodbye to Mother Adriel, boys. I need you home."

"So long Mother Adriel," Hammen said sadly.

"Bye," Toller said curtly, heading towards the trees.

Yolta grabbed her eldest son's shoulder and turned him to face Adriel. "Toller! Show Mother Adriel proper respect."

"It's all right, Yolta," Adriel assured the woman.

"No. My boys need to learn the proper respect that must be paid to an enchantress." Yolta turned her attention to her two boys and adopted a lecturing tone. "One day, when Mother Olla is gone, Mother Adriel here will be the one we turn to when we need enchantments for our gardening equipment, wards for our home, or need soothing runestones for when your wives' bear children. Now, Toller, show the enchantress proper respect."

Toller grunted, his eyes never leaving the ground. "Goodbye, Mother Adriel."

Adriel thought the lecture was a bit much, but she wasn't about to criticize Yolta's mothering—if the boys must learn respect, it was up to her to decide how. She smiled at the boy and mussed his hair gently. "I'll see you soon." Toller turned and headed into the trees, towards his family's cabin.

"You too, Hammen," Yolta added.

"Toller said *fucking*," Hammen blurted out before running off after his brother. His mother's eyebrows shot up in bewilderment. Adriel chuckled.

"Those boys," Yolta muttered. "I hate to say it, but they're the mirror image of their father when he was young. Our family homes were on the same tenure, so my brothers and I would play with him. You should have seen the teasing he would give me. When his father found out he had thrown rocks at the neighbors' girl, True One knows he got a switching worth a lifetime. He never teased me again after that."

"It's hard to imagine Brade as that sort of child," Adriel said, the feather twirling between her hands.

"Aye. He was very different back then. Now he's all about his labor, not that I'm complaining. We want for nothing, and it's mostly because of Brade's hard work." Yolta's eyes fell upon the feather, its reflected light making her already bright eyes appear even brighter. Adriel smiled and handed the feather to the woman. Yolta examined it carefully as if it were a treasure of unquantifiable worth. "My granny had one just like it. Said her mother had given it to her. It was one of the few things she was burned with when she passed. A *melk* feather." It wasn't a question, but Adriel nodded in response. "My granny used to tell me stories from her mother's childhood. Terrible, bloody, stories about those vicious things wiping out entire tenures in a single night."

"Perhaps she was simply trying to scare you so you would behave. Like stories of weaselbogs and the shadowfolk."

Yolta shook her head. "Not these stories, the way my granny told them. Said the *melk* were pushed out of Albadone after a long week's hunt, but those who remember have long passed." Yolta returned the feather to Adriel with a small sigh. "I'm sure Mother Olla knows something about it if you ask her."

"I'll do just that when I return home." Adriel carefully placed the feather in her satchel. Yolta's eyes stayed on it until it was completely out of sight.

"Please give Mother Olla my best regards. And do stop by for dinner some time, the both of you. I'll make roasted boar and black berry tarts. Oh, and I have a fresh batch of spiced wine that will warm you to the bone."

Adriel bowed her head slightly in thanks. "You're too kind, Yolta. I'll make sure to let Mother Olla know." Yolta returned the bow and flashed a smile so quickly that it might have only been in Adriel's imagination. The baby wrapped around Yolta's chest began to squirm and fuss. The young mother gently shushed the child as she headed towards her home.

The sun was finally warming the late morning air. Adriel pulled back her hood revealing a mess of brown curls that were barely corralled into a ponytail behind her head by an unfortunate sliver of ribbon. She wiped the dampness off her neck, and proceeded deeper into the woods, eastward from where Yolta and her children were headed. She conjured a list in her mind of all of Mother Olla's tomes she had read, hoping to recall some clue as to which one contained information regarding *melk*. There was so much information in those tomes, and often she found herself skimming paragraphs or skipping chapters entirely, especially those on boring subjects. She loved reading on higher enchanting, but the chapters on runesmithing drove her to sleep. Mother Olla had swatted at her head and called her "lazybones" when she caught her skipping a chapter or dozing off.

"Runesmithing is the most essential part of enchanting," the old woman scolded. "How is a seamstress supposed to sew without string? A blacksmith craft a sword without iron?" Adriel knew her teacher was right, but nothing could make reading about that subject any more endurable.

The cabin was about four miles from Chanter's Hill, and it took until midday for her to reach it. It stood in an almost perfectly circular clearing—'stood' wasn't quite the right word to describe the dilapidated state of the cabin. Mother

Olla claimed that it was built three hundred years past using wood from an ancient wishing tree that was cut down after a king's poorly phrased wish caused his first-born to die. Adriel thought that story was a nonsense excuse for Mother Olla to avoid having the cabin rebuilt. The windows were drafty, and the roof was leaky when it rained, causing the floorboards to rot in certain spots. The musty smell of soft decaying wood pervaded every corner of the cabin. Even the tomes in the library smelled like old dirt, their pages warped from water damage several decades old. The less time Adriel spent in the cabin the better. She preferred to study outside in the fresh air anyway.

As she made her way to the cabin, she passed by the *spyrale*, a peculiar installation of runestones Mother Olla said predated the cabin by at least several hundred years—Adriel was sure the old woman often exaggerated dates to give certain things the illusion of being more important than they truly were. The *spyrale* was comprised of fifty or so dead runestones—gray runestones whose magic had been fully utilized—splayed artfully on the ground in a spiral shape. Adriel had to admit that the runestones towards the center of the *spyrale* did look quite old, their runic symbols erased by the elements, but several hundred years seemed a stretch. Mother Olla had never actually explained what the use of the *spyrale* was but, based on the whisper of *life energy* emanating from it, Adriel assumed they functioned as a sort of *Warding*. When she had asked, Mother Olla always dismissed or ignored the question—the old woman hated being caught not knowing something.

A black cloud arose from the chimney. Mother Olla had begun performing whatever enchantment she was working on. If Adriel didn't hurry in with the *poxcheeks* she knew she would receive a switching to rival Brade's.

II.

THE CABIN

The black smoke enveloping the inside of the cramped cabin rushed to escape through the front door. The smell of scorched leather was almost strong enough to cover the dank rot of the floorboards. Adriel rushed inside, keeping the door open behind her to clear the air, and made her way through the thick smoke. Mother Olla stood in front of the lit fireplace struggling to hold her grip on a pair of rusty iron tongs—her pale slim arms buckled under their weight. Adriel hurried to the old woman and took the tongs from her. The source of the smoke was a small leather pouch, which lay charred in the fireplace underneath a large cauldron. Adriel reached for the pouch with the tongs, carefully attempting to pull it out of the fire. It was too late for the pouch's contents, which lay black and unrecognizable among the bright flames.

"This is what happens when you take too long to return," the old woman complained, her low leveled voice masking any sort of emotion—that's how Adriel knew she was frustrated.

"I'm here now, aren't I?" Adriel shook her head. "You could have waited—"

The old woman whacked Adriel on the back of her head with her bony hand—a familiar sting. Where was this strength when it came to holding the tongs?

Adriel bit her lip. "I'm sorry, Mother Olla." The young woman finally managed to get a good grip on the burning pouch, dragging it out of the fire and onto the floor. She dropped the tongs, Mother Olla grimacing as the iron hit the floor—as if she cared about the state of the cabin—and picked up a small pot from a hook dangling overhead. She quickly placed the pot over the smoking bundle, smothering the flames. When Adriel looked up, Mother Olla had already moved to her workbench on the other side of the room as if nothing had happened.

"You have my mushrooms." It wasn't a question. The old woman held her left hand out awaiting the *poxcheeks* while rummaging through a toolbox with her right. Adriel pulled the small sack from her satchel, which she still wore, and placed it onto Mother Olla's hand. The woman raised the sack up and down, considering. "Heavy," was all she said. She didn't use many words if one or two could convey her meanings.

"I picked a few extra mushrooms, just in case—"

"In case what?" the woman fumed, every wrinkle on her face tensing into a mask of anger. "In case I drop them into the fireplace as I did with those damned fishbones?"

Adriel lowered her head. If she didn't apologize again soon, a slap on the back of the head would be the least of her troubles. "I'm sorry, Mother Olla, I didn't mean to—"

"BAH!" Mother Olla spat on the floor—another one of the old woman's habits Adriel could do without. "Keep your false apologies to yourself and help me out, will you? Had I those strong young arms of yours I would have everything done by now." The old woman fiddled with the pendant around her neck: a yellow runestone with the cross shape of *Binding* carved onto it. Mother Olla only ever wore plain clothes and no other jewelry, so Adriel knew the pendant's true function was to cover the deep ragged scar that encircled her neck—Adriel had always known better than to ask about the scar. "And close the damned door! It's bloody cold out there."

Adriel did as the old woman commanded, then set her satchel onto her bed—a small, hay-stuffed, cot in the far corner of the room, by the draftiest window—and quickly made her way towards Mother Olla's workbench in the middle of the cabin. The workbench was a large smooth black stone with a flattened surface that shimmered in the sunlight—it had been carved from a piece of the Womb of the World. How the old woman had gotten that in here was beyond her. The workbench functioned as a vessel that channeled the *life energy* of the woods surrounding the cabin, concentrating it into one place. Being near it, feeling the *life energy* make its way under her skin, filling her lungs, was the only good part about being in that wretched cabin.

On the right side of the workbench was the 'library'—five crooked and wobbling shelves stacked with dusty old handwritten tomes—while to the left of it was a bulky dresser, its drawers filled with runestones, both crafted and raw. Other than the workbench, the dresser was the item that stood out the most in the cabin. It was well built, almost too well, with silver finishing and beautiful floral carvings climbing up its sides like ivy. Compared to Adriel's shabby cot, and Mother Olla's even shabbier one, the dresser seemed gaudy even. Where such a flashy item had come from, Mother Olla had never provided an answer.

The old woman set the pouch of mushrooms on the workbench and produced a thick golden needle from the toolbox, setting it next to the pouch. She slowly got to her knees in front of the bookshelves, her knobby joints popping in multiple places as she did so, and pulled out a small wooden box from underneath, the carving of a fox on its lid long rotted away. She lifted it towards Adriel, fully expecting the young woman to know exactly what she needed. Adriel knew the woman well, so she took the box from her and helped her to her feet. "Seven fishbones wrapped in blessed leather," she explained. "Boiled for the duration of a *Sealing* chant."

Adriel nodded and got to work. She set the box onto the small desk at the foot of her bed—a pitiful little thing with one leg shorter than the other three—and opened it, revealing an assortment of fish parts: bones, scales, eyes, tails... She carefully picked out the seven best looking bones and set them aside. She reached for a drawer on the right side of the desk and pulled it open, to some resistance; the sound of wood scraping on wood made her grit her teeth. Inside were several sheets of thin leather neatly stacked on top of each other. She picked one sheet out and wrapped the fishbones in it.

"Make sure you don't use any twine," the old woman called out.

"Yes, Mother," Adriel answered, knowing fully well how it was done. She did her best to tie the pouch without string, and then picked up the iron tongs that were left on the floor in front of the fireplace. With the tongs, she picked up the leather pouch from the desk and raised it above the cauldron—the water inside had been boiling for a while it seemed. Adriel took a deep breath and placed the pouch into the water, holding it carefully under the bubbling surface. "*Adouns, melliat, endergo,*" she chanted solemnly. "*Adouns, olle mandango foth ut einte, endergo.*" Mother Olla had often been very critical of Adriel as a student of the enchanting arts—Adriel, too, admitted that she fell short many a time. But if there was one subject she had always excelled in, it was *Chanter's Tongue*, the language of the True One. Mother Olla said her special connection to nature and her ability to sense *life energy* facilitated her learning the language, as *life energy* itself was an extension of the True One's hand. Adriel didn't understand most of it but was glad there was at least one subject she was good at.

When the chant had concluded, she immediately pulled the fishbones out of the water and made her way towards the workbench. Carefully, she set the pouch on the smooth black surface of the stone. Wisps of vapor lifted into the air as the hot wet leather touched the cool dry stone. Mother Olla unfastened the pouch, unflinching at the heat, to reveal the wet fishbones. She carefully pulled out all seven, laying them in front of her in order of length.

Adriel set the tongs on a hook on the wall next to the fireplace. "Yolta and Brade invited us over for dinner," she said casually.

"Brade..." The old woman said the name as if it were a curse. "Have you seen that horrid thing he and those men have been building? It's an affront to the True One and nature itself. I've had dreams and visions about it and not the good sort." Adriel rolled her eyes, thankful that Mother Olla's back was facing her. The old enchantress was sorting through the pouch, placing the best-looking *poxcheeks* in a neat pile next to the fishbones. Adriel rummaged through her satchel, producing the *melk* feather. Speckles of sunlight danced around the room as she twirled it. "What do you have there?" Mother Olla asked.

"I found it on Chanter's Hill," the young woman said, making her way towards the workbench.

Mother Olla slowly turned towards Adriel, her eyes set on the feather, her work seemingly forgotten. "A *melk* feather?" she said slowly. "And a beautiful one, too. Intact. It's been a long while since I've seen a *melk* in these woods. Up on Chanter's Hill, you say?"

Something in the way the old woman spoke troubled Adriel, although she couldn't say why. "Yes, Mother."

The old woman carefully reached for the feather, as if it were hotter than the boiled leather she so casually unwrapped moments before. She held the feather with a strange solemnity, lightly running her fingers across its length. "Peculiar," she said. "Could be an omen. Thank you for this wonderful gift, child." Mother Olla placed the feather in her hair and returned to her work. Adriel looked at her and the feather in confusion. She had never seen Mother Olla place anything in her hair, not even a Spring blossom. The feather was an unexpected jewel in the nest of untamed gray-white tufts on the woman's head.

While the woman was busy working over the enchantment, Adriel turned her attention towards the bookshelves. She scanned the spines of the messily stacked tomes until she reached a particular one that she was sure contained what she was looking for. "*Minor Enchantments and Deities, Volume II*" contained a catalog of ingredients that didn't require chanting to awaken their *life energy*. She was certain she had seen the picture of the *melk* feather in there somewhere. She flipped through the brown warped pages, past list after list, most written by at least four different hands. Some entries were accompanied by pictures—those also drawn by a few different artists—some artistically rendered, with shading and color, while others were rudimentary and, at times, unrecognizable as anything other than scribbles. Finally, she found what she was searching for, about two-thirds of the way through the tome: a recreation of the *melk* feather exactly as it appeared in reality. She read quietly:

"*When gifted, the* melk *feather's life energy will awaken, casting a protective spell on the recipient of the gift. Perfect as a wedding gift.*"

That sneaky old witch, Adriel thought to herself. *A gift, she called it.* The old woman still managed to surprise Adriel with her cleverness, even after all these years. She may be old and frail in appearance, but her mind was sharp as a wasp stinger.

"Well look who's studying without being asked," Mother Olla said, almost mockingly. Adriel's cheeks reddened. With the golden needle, the old woman stitched the seven mushrooms together in a circle with iron thread before stabbing each mushroom through with a fishbone. She set the strange creation onto a flat piece of undyed wool cloth. "There was a time when I had to force you to do many things, studying and reading especially. It was almost as if you wanted me to take you back to the gutter where I found you, not that the thought never crossed my mind." Adriel sighed and closed the book, setting it back on the shelf in no particular place. "Thank the True One you've grown into the fine young woman you are. Well, thanks to me mostly." Mother Olla looked over at Adriel, smirking at her soured expression. "I'm just teasing, child."

"Oh, I know, Mother," Adriel replied sullenly.

"Do learn to take a joke." Mother Olla pulled out a piece of undyed string, tying the cloth with it. The old woman turned to face Adriel, who attempted to transform her grimace into a smile. Mother Olla shook her head. "Adriel, are you really going to make me do this? You know you're as a daughter to me. I'm only hard on you because I see your true potential. I might have a hard time showing it but," the old woman paused as if weighing her words carefully. "I'm proud of you. I know that when my body dies, you'll take good care of all I've built."

Adriel stood stunned, staring at the old woman as if for the first time. "I'm grateful, Mother," was all she could muster.

"You better be," Mother Olla said, returning to her normal self. "Now, perform a *Blessing* chant on these while I go take a shit." Adriel suppressed a laugh and made her way to the bench. Mother Olla opened the front door of the cabin and walked out, leaving the door open behind her. *So much for letting a draft in.* Adriel reached into a small canister, pulling out a handful of coarse pink salt. She drew a circle with the salt around the cloth pouch and began chanting with her eyes closed. "*Adouns, melliat, endergo. Ke olle mandango settu ut elle mek...*" Her hands hovered over the pouch, as *life energy* began to pour into it from the workbench.

The *Blessing* chant was the first one she had ever learned. To her surprise, it took only a few repetitions for her to have it completely memorized. The words felt natural as if conjured from a deep part of her soul, almost as if she had always known them. Mother Olla taught her that the True One spoke the chants into all life at the beginning of time, but that only some could remember. Every time the old woman had taught her a new chant, no matter its use, Adriel always felt that same feeling: a sort of ecstatic glee at having remembered something she didn't know she had forgotten. It was a feeling she loved and had continued to chase until Mother Olla had told her there were no more chants to learn besides the Seven. That broke her heart. Surely there were more. There had to be.

"*Perhaps you don't know them all*" she pleaded to the old woman. That cost her a smack that made her inner cheek bleed. She was a child then, who didn't know better. She knew now not to push the old woman and especially not to tell her she didn't know enough.

After seven repetitions of the chant, Adriel placed her hand on the salt circle and, with a quick swipe, broke it. Behind her, she heard the sound of footsteps entering the cabin. "I've finished the chant, Mother." Adriel picked up the small cloth sack and turned. But it wasn't Mother Olla who had entered the cabin. A young man in full plated armor, helmet under his arm, stood at the open door.

Adriel *gasped*.

III.
A Visitor

The gray overcast sky kept the midday sun at bay resulting in a much cooler day than usual, even for the middle of an already colder-than-usual Autumn. The gentle breeze blowing through the open door sent goosebumps crawling down Adriel's spine. But it wasn't the chill that kept her frozen still.

The man at the door was the most handsome she had ever seen; in all fairness, she hadn't seen many in her life other than the neighboring woodsmen—barrel-chested men with hairy arms and unkempt beards—or the occasional leathery merchant on his way to nearby towns. This young man was nothing like that sort. His straight, dirt-blonde, locks fell loosely about his shoulders, a neatly cut fringe kissing the bushy eyebrows above his piercing blue eyes. His jaw was angular, and his smile was soft and enchanting, albeit uncomfortable at this very moment.

The blue cross marking on his barely-worn chest plate indicated he was an errant knight: a free agent that took any and all work for a reward, from protecting livestock during travel to rescuing damsels in distress—although Adriel was sure that only ever happened in stories. His gauntleted hand instinctually hovered over the steel pommel of his sword, which was sheathed in a surprisingly ornate leather scabbard at his hip. In his other hand was a leather satchel, not too dissimilar from her own.

The young man's blue cloak snapped angrily as the wind outside picked up. It was then that Adriel realized the man had been speaking to her—for how long, she hadn't the faintest idea. "I'm sorry. I didn't mean to frighten you," he said placidly. "The door was open, and I..." He let the sentence dangle in the air unfinished.

Adriel slowly filled her lungs with the biting air and put on her best smile. It seemed the man was just as uneasy as she was, which made her feel somewhat better. "It's all right," she said. "I'm Adriel. How may I be of service?"

The young man's tension slowly vanished, his hand relaxing away from his sword. "I'm searching for an enchantress named Mother Olla. Do you know where I may find her?"

"And who in *Ulfer's* arse might you be?" Mother Olla's phlegmy voice came from outside. The young man turned to find the old woman standing a few feet behind him tapping her foot impatiently, hands at her hips. The silver feather in her hair shone, although the sun was hidden behind a thick layer of graying clouds. The young man's eyes were drawn to it immediately.

"You must be her!" the man intoned excitedly as he made his way out of the cabin. Adriel followed him and stood next to Mother Olla, who tilted her head, awaiting more from the young errant knight. "I heard you are the greatest and most powerful—"

"—and most wonderful, and beautiful, and all that," she interrupted. "I am very aware of who I am, child. But I am yet to be introduced to whoever you might be."

The man shook his head, in part in recoil from Mother Olla's sharp tongue, and in part from forgetting his manners. He dropped onto one knee as quickly as his heavy armor would allow. "Pardons mistress. My name is Yugo. I am a warrior for hire, an errant knight, from the city of Vizen. I recently completed a quest for Thane Bovieu, which left me quite a bit richer than I was before, if you catch my meaning." By his tone and the grin that grew on his face, it appeared Yugo had made a joke. By Mother Olla's face, it was clear she hated every word out of the young man's mouth.

"Let me guess," she spat, "you want me to enchant your undergarments with a runestone of *shit-no-more*?" Adriel snorted. The man laughed as well, but only out of politeness. He slowly stood up, struggling under the weight of the clunky armor.

"Our rate is two gold pieces for blessed twine, and five pieces for a runestone enchantment," Adriel explained. "We also have some runestones for sale if you'd like to take them to an enchanter elsewhere. We craft them ourselves right here and they are of the highest quality."

"No need," Yugo reached inside his satchel. "I already have a rune of my own." After digging for a while, he produced the smoothest runestone—was that thing even a runestone?—Adriel had ever seen. It was a shimmering black sphere, the half-moon shape of *Power* etched onto it. It was unclear if the soft glow of the black stone was merely a reflection of the light of day or if it was produced by the sphere itself. As Adriel ran her thumb over the runic symbol—it seemed to her as if it was etched *within* the stone under a thin layer of glass. Stranger still was that Adriel couldn't feel any energy emanating from it, as if it lay dormant or was already spent. But the etching on the stone was still intact, which meant that whatever the stone's enchanting properties were, they were still very much alive and usable.

Mother Olla moved in closer, eying the runestone suspiciously. "Wherever did you find such a thing?" she asked.

"There I was," Yugo began with a bright smile, his voice deepening in that way storytellers' did when diving into an epic tale. "My team and I were separated, when—"

"Spare me the details," Mother Olla swatted, irritated. "Some of us have work to tend to. Where did you find it?"

Yugo cleared his throat, his eagerness to tell his—no doubt—self-flattering tale melting away. "It was among a *Reaverlord's* treasures. I arrived late after my team killed it. They looted all the gold and diamonds. Thankfully, Lord Bovieu's reward for clearing his fields made up for it. The sole thing my team left behind, besides a couple of rare manuscripts I managed to sell, was this runestone. Please, tell me, is it worth anything?"

"I wonder where a filthy *Reaverlord* got its hands on such a thing. Give it here, child." The old woman held out her bony hand. Yugo handed her the runestone and she began to examine it. By her expressions, Adriel could tell it was one of the rarest runestones the old woman had ever seen—perhaps even one of the rarest runestones in existence. Mother Olla ran her fingers across the smooth surface of the stone with a puzzled expression. Every once in a while, she put it to her ear, hoping to hear or feel something—what, Adriel hadn't the faintest. She even went as far as licking it at one point, to which Yugo wrinkled his nose. Adriel wasn't sure what that was supposed to accomplish either, but she never questioned the old woman's methods.

"Ten gold pieces," Mother Olla announced.

Adriel raised an eyebrow. The old woman had overcharged men before, especially when they came from the city or if she didn't like their face, but ten gold pieces was an outrageous cost. Even Yugo gave pause.

"Mother, why so much?" Adriel asked.

Mother Olla shot daggers at Adriel, then quickly looked back at the knight as if the young woman hadn't said a word. "It'll take time, as well. It's definitely a runestone, but not of any sort I have ever seen before. It'll take a fortnight, perhaps more, to study it thoroughly and prepare it for enchanting."

"A fortnight!" Yugo exclaimed, outraged. "I don't have that long. There's a warrior's tourney at the Palace in four days to commemorate Prince Hovard's second birthday. I was hoping to have my armor or sword enchanted by then."

"With this runestone? Impossible," was all Mother Olla said. She slammed the black runestone into Yugo's hand and walked past him into the cabin. As far as she was concerned, the transaction was over. Yugo stood there dumbfounded for a moment, before turning his attention to Adriel. The young woman shrugged and shook her head. Mother Olla quickly returned to the doorway, pointing an accusing finger at the knight. "And do not dare ask my apprentice to do anything for you, unless you have a hankering for a swift kick in the groin." With that, she slammed the door to the cabin.

"Why can't she just do it?" Yugo asked Adriel quietly, clearly afraid to be heard by the old woman. In a challenge of strength, Yugo would have been able to overtake the old woman without breaking so much as a sweat. But Mother Olla had a way of instilling fear and unease into even the bravest of men.

"If we don't know what sort of runestone it is, we risk breaking it during the enchantment," Adriel explained. "Even worse, a wrong ingredient or a wrong chant could have adverse effects upon the wearer of the enchantment. It is by far the most unique runestone I have ever seen, and even Mother Olla seemed surprised by it, which is very telling. Truly, it is for your safety."

"I see," he said, puzzling out something in his head. "So, you care for my safety?" Yugo put on a gallant grin, the sort that Adriel was sure worked wonders on naïve woodsfolk girls, but perhaps not as well on the city ones. He was beautiful, she had to admit, but his arrogance spoke of a life of privilege, one much different from hers.

"I'm sorry, Yugo," she apologized. "Have a pleasant day." Adriel opened the door and made her way inside. Before she could close the door, Yugo shoved his booted foot inside, blocking it with a thud.

"Enchantress!" he yelled. Adriel jumped, startled. "Ten gold pieces, you say? I'll pay double if you perform the enchantment right now. If I feared for my safety what sort of errant knight would I be?" The braggadocio oozed from every word.

Olla walked to the door, her face darkened by irritation, and pushed Adriel aside. "What a foolish pea-brained thing to say. Besides, there are many other enchantresses in Albadone, even some in your smelly Vizen, that would be more than happy to take your gold."

Yugo shook his head, his smile unwavering. "But I don't want just any enchantress. I want the best of the best: you. I've heard the name *Olla* spoken as far as Rondhill. I've met a King's Knight with an enchanted sword that could slice through steel as if made of pure flame. You did that for him, he said. I want that power. You can give me that power." Mother Olla shook her head and swatted the young man away as if he were nothing but a pesky gnat. "I'll pay you three—no, four times, forty gold pieces if you perform the enchantment right now."

Adriel felt bile rising at the back of her throat. Forty gold pieces? Surely this man was mad. That was as much gold as they made in a typical year. With that amount, she could not only have the cabin rebuilt, but build a second, perhaps even a third, cabin right next door. To an onlooker, Mother Olla's face might have appeared unperturbed, but Adriel knew her better than anyone else. Deep down, the old woman was as shocked by the proposition as she was. By the crack in his voice, Yugo sounded equally unsure of his own words.

"You're mad, child," Olla said as she ruminated on the offer. Then, after a deep sigh, she nodded. "Forty, not one gold piece less." Yugo smiled wide, but there was regret hiding plainly behind his eyes. "Don't touch anything." The old woman disappeared into the cabin. Adriel held the door open to let Yugo inside.

The knight looked around the cabin, his nose wrinkling, no doubt because of the thick stench of wood rot. Adriel held her palm towards him, and he handed her the runestone. She set it on the workbench. Mother Olla sat on a tall stool in front of the workbench, and gently fingered the black runestone.

Adriel approached the knight and said, "We require payment in advance." When Yugo raised an eyebrow she continued, "Payment is part of the enchantment. Enchantments always require a cost, and the gold you give us is used in the channeling of *life energy*, so that the enchanted object may resonate with you."

"When you're done with the lesson, draw a salt circle around the house and perform a *Warding* chant seven times," Mother Olla interjected. "We must take every precaution."

"Yes, Mother," Adriel answered.

Yugo reached into his satchel and pulled out a heavy pouch. He unlaced it, revealing several gold pieces. He pulled out ten and tossed them back into the satchel, then handed over the pouch to Adriel. "That's forty," he said with the tone of someone who had just lost everything.

Adriel gave him a reassuring smile, set the pouch on the workbench, and headed to the far corner of the cabin, past the bookshelves, where raw ingredients were stored. She chose a particular unlabeled brown sack from a pile of other indistinguishable sacks. It was much too heavy to carry, so she slowly dragged it towards the front door.

"May I be of assistance?" Yugo asked, nearing Adriel.

"No!" Mother Olla raised a finger in the air. "If she can't carry that out, her body won't grow strong, and she'll be asking men in armor for help her whole life."

Adriel sighed as Yugo backed away towards the cots on the far end of the room. Adriel let go of the sack and picked up her satchel from her bed. "You can sit here if you'd like." Yugo shot her a friendly smile—maybe a bit more than friendly, or was she imagining it?—and sat on Adriel's lumpy cot.

On the workbench, near the toolbox were several vials of scented liquids, each of a different color and consistency. Mother Olla uncorked a vial and gave its thin green contents a sniff. She dampened a clean undyed cloth with the green liquid and rubbed it across the surface of the runestone until it was bright and shiny. She placed the vial back in its place and reached for the toolbox, from which she produced a golden needle.

Yugo yawned casually. "So, what is it that you're—"

"Please tell me you don't plan on speaking the entire time," Mother Olla admonished impatiently. Yugo quieted and watched as Adriel dragged the sack outside.

The wind had calmed a bit, but the clouds had thickened enough to lower the temperature considerably. Adriel dragged the sack across the dirt in front of the cabin. She stopped after a few feet to catch her breath and stretch her sore arms. She really could have used the knight's help, but the old woman was fixated on self-reliance. The life of an enchantress was often a lonely one, and if an enchantress wasn't able to complete a physical task on her own perhaps it wasn't the life for her. But to refuse help from someone who offered it seemed silly. As usual, she avoided any sort of unnecessary confrontation with the old woman. Once she had limbered up, she opened the mouth of the sack revealing coarse pink salt—the same that filled the canister atop the workbench. Carefully, she tilted the sack until salt piled on the ground. Slowly she dragged the salt sack forming a pink circle around the cabin. Once she was finished, the sack was almost emptied. She wiped a crown of sweat and ensured that no part of the circle was broken, or the *Warding* enchantment wouldn't take hold.

"*Adouns, melliat, tropekto,*" she intoned solemnly, beginning the first *Warding* chant. "*Tropekto, melliat, sentro foth ut ente, tropekto.*" She repeated the chant seven times, careful to enunciate each word and to maintain an even speed. "It is finished!" she exclaimed a few moments after the last chant. By then, Mother Olla would have had the ingredients for the enchantment readied. She would hammer a golden pick through the etching in the runestone, releasing its power. It was a procedure Adriel had witnessed countless times—and done herself a half dozen. The last time she had done it, however, she accidentally shattered the runestone. The old woman had furiously smacked the back of her head and vowed it would be a year and a day before she would perform another enchantment. It had been eight months since then.

From inside, Adriel heard the hammer hitting the pick with a decisive metal *clink*, and the runestone cracking underneath.

Then silence.

Inside, the fire in the fireplace blew out. Yugo fell from the cot onto the ground with a limp thud and lay there unmoving and unblinking. Something was terribly wrong. The clouds above the cabin turned black and angry.

"Mother!" Adriel cried out. "Mother!" She called out again and again, to no reply. She stood at the very edge of the salt circle, not daring to cross it or else risk releasing whatever evil had been unleashed by the black runestone. Anxiety bubbled in her stomach as she awaited something, anything. She ran to the side of the cabin to peek through the window, but she couldn't get near enough to get a good look inside. She ran again to the front door. A thin voice cried out indiscernibly from inside the cabin as if coming from a deep dark hole. It was the old woman.

"Mother Olla! Can you hear me?" Adriel asked, fear balling her hands into tight fists.

"Child..." the woman whimpered. Mother Olla's face peeked out from the side of the doorway as she crawled across the floor into view. Adriel instinctively stepped towards the door, forgetting the salt circle. "Stop!" the old woman howled, barely sounding like herself.

"A curse?" Adriel asked, already knowing the answer.

"A strong one," Mother Olla replied slowly. "I've been touched by it, but not fully. Thanks to you."

"Thanks to me?" Adriel asked confused. Tears welled up in her eyes. She had never seen the old woman in such a feeble and contorted state.

"Your gift."

It took but a moment for Adriel to understand. The sentence from "*Minor Enchantments and Deities, Volume II*" she had read earlier manifested in her mind. Gifting the *melk* feather to the old woman—rather, the old woman accepting the feather as a gift—had awakened the feather's enchanting properties. It warded Mother Olla from the curse. But its protection could only do so much.

"*Turtlewig* thorns, *whitecaps*, black earth!" Mother Olla coughed the words out as clearly as she was able. "Bring them here at once.

"A cure?" Adriel asked. The old woman nodded. Adriel repeated the list of ingredients to herself a few times until she had them memorized. "Are you going to be all right here? Should I get help?"

"Go!" Mother Olla said. Even in her state she sounded commanding. As soon as Adriel turned to leave, the old woman shouted, "Wait! Adriel!"

Adriel faced the woman, doing her best to hide her fear. No, it wasn't fear. It was terror. "Yes, Mother?" she asked, her voice as steady as she could force it.

Mother Olla licked her thin dry lips and reached for the yellow runestone around her neck with a trembling hand. "I trust you, child."

Adriel nodded and hurried into the deep woods, repeating the three ingredients to herself over and over.

IV.

THE HUNT

"*Turtlewig* thorns, *whitecaps*, black earth! *Turtlewig* thorns, *whitecaps*, black earth!" Adriel repeated the ingredients to herself in a shaky voice, fearing that stopping would let them vanish from her mind. She ran through the woods, at first in no particular direction. Her thoughts were scattered and frozen; all she could focus on were the names of the ingredients and nothing else. As her mind slowly cleared, she realized she was running towards the Chleo, the river where Mother Olla sent her to fetch water every other day. The current was strong here, the thin river bubbling where it hit the smooth white stones that lined its banks. She soon realized she hadn't formulated a plan of action other than '*run*'. As she cried, her weak legs collapsed beneath her.

'*Mother*' was the old woman's title as an enchantress, and everyone referred to her as such in reverence. But to Adriel, the word was more than a mere title. The woman was the only family Adriel had, and the only mother she had ever known. She had faint memories of a faceless father, and many faceless brothers and sisters; a Winter so biting that she survived by hiding among the bodies of her dead family; wandering the woods aimlessly, days and nights massing together in a blur of pain and survival. It was a hazy dream—or a nightmare, truly—that didn't seem quite real anymore. Her most concrete memory was Mother Olla, walking her to the cabin, the woman's warm hand holding hers. She remembered the warmth of a fire, and the smell of a stew cooking; the old woman soothing her blue fingers and toes. Mother Olla could be hard on her, even cruel at times, but she took her in and cared for her as her own daughter. Losing the old woman would mean losing her family. It would mean being alone again.

"Enough!" she admonished herself between sobs. "Mother needs you now. This is the time to prove yourself to her." Adriel took a few deep breaths to steady herself. She crawled to the river and drove her hand into the frigid water, wiping away the tears and dirt from her face. The cold bite of the water awakened her senses. She stood to her feet, with new determination.

"*Turtlewig* thorns, *whitecaps*, black earth," she repeated. She looked at her surroundings, thinking about where the nearest ingredient may be. "*Turtlewigs* and *whitecaps* grow by water." She wiped the dirt from her knees, and hurried along, following the riverbed. *Whitecaps* would be easiest to find, but *Turtlewig* bushes only flowered in the Spring. Thankfully, she needed the thorns and not the blossoms, but even those could prove hard to spot in Autumn. She decided to follow the bank north-west. She recalled seeing those bushes grow there a few Springs ago. *Turtlewig* wasn't an ingredient for many enchantments—she couldn't recall the reason they had needed them last. She hoped she was correct about their whereabouts, else she would be following the river in vain.

To her delight, about a mile from where she had started, she discovered several graying thorny bushes growing where the river widened. She examined the nearest bush: the dust-colored dead petals mixed with the dirt at the base of the plant confirmed these were *Turtlewigs*—the blossoms were light blue in the Spring but quickly turned gray when picked. She unsheathed her dagger and cut off a thick and fibrous stem, which proved a challenge. When it finally released, she carefully set it in her satchel.

"Two more to go," she assured herself, her confidence growing. "Now, for the *whitecaps*. Those grow by the river as well, but on trees." Following the trail of *Turtlewigs*, she had walked into a more sparsely wooded area. The trees surrounding her were dried up and dormant—*whitecaps* needed moisture. She looked across to the other side of the river, where the foliage was thick with evergreens—their *life energy* was weak but still very much awake. She sighed and reluctantly made her way across the frigid water. At its deepest, it reached her calves, but the numbness caused by the freezing water was almost too much to bear. Despite the biting sting, Adriel kept moving.

By the time she reached the opposite bank, she was shaking uncontrollably, her breath coming out in grunts through gritted teeth. Wading through the river was not the smartest plan, but her options were limited, and her time was running short. She hurried towards the nearby trees, her legs made out of lead. She moved from tree to tree with no luck. After the tenth tree, her heart began beating anxiously and her breathing quickened. Then ten became fifteen, and fifteen became twenty. There was no sign of the mushrooms anywhere. She was panting by this point, a distressed warmth reddening her face.

"Please, oh please," she begged to no one in particular. *Whitecaps* weren't a common ingredient either. Unlike *poxcheek* mushrooms, *whitecaps* were poisonous, causing one's blood to quickly turn to jelly. *Warding* and *Transference* were its two enchanting properties she remembered, having read them in a book, but she had never actually used them in an enchantment before.

As she uttered her plea, she was reminded of when she was a girl. Mother Olla would take her on walks through the woods to test her perception of *life energy*. Some days, the old woman would blindfold her and ask her to find her way back home—a few times alone. Other times, she would let Adriel touch an ingredient and then ask her to locate it in the woods. She vaguely remembered having to track down *whitecaps* once, but the memory was fuzzy. She recalled being on her knees reaching for them and going in for a bite— even as a girl she had loved the taste of mushrooms—when Mother Olla slapped them out of her hand, warning her about their deadly poison. *Wait!* She remembered reaching for them from her knees. *Of course!*

Whitecaps grew on trees near the river, but not on their trunks: they grew under their roots. Adriel smiled and ran to the nearest tree. She bent to her knees and began digging through the wet dirt until she exposed a thick system of large, knotted roots. There they were: small white ball-like mushroom caps. Giddy with excitement, she ripped the mushrooms from the roots and placed them into her satchel. Then she moved to another tree and dug for more. She wanted as many as she could get her hands on. She had been scolded for picking too many *poxcheeks* earlier that day, but she would not run the risk of having too few *whitecaps*. By the time she was done, she must have had at least thirty of them in her satchel. Energized, she stood up, unworried by her muddy hood, and set forth.

The black earth was the only ingredient she knew for certain where to find, but it was the one that would take the most effort. Over the years, she and Mother Olla had gone to fill sacks with it, but the trek was long, and dragging those sacks required a cart and at least two mules, which they rented from Pevine, the nearest town at the western outskirts of the forest. Adriel knew they had a sack full of it back at the cabin, but it had been a year since they had gathered it, so her assumption was that the old woman required fresh black earth. Mother Olla had not been clear on how much of it was required, so she was sure a few fistfuls would be enough. She would have to cross the Chleo again, but she would do it where the river wasn't so wide or deep. After crossing, her feet already numb to the sharpness of the icy cold water, she turned south and out of the forest, towards the Womb of the World.

An hour passed before any changes in terrain were apparent. First, the trees grew sparser, and eventually, the earth itself changed from brown and muddy to rocky and coarse. Adriel's legs had thawed out, but she still felt the air grow colder as the terrain inclined upwards, and after a few miles she could see the tops of the trees below, and even Chanter's Hill and that strange wooden structure in the distance. A few hundred paces later, the incline turned to a downhill slope, leading to a small circular valley where the rocky terrain turned into rich black earth. The vegetation here was sparse except for those strange thorny plants Mother Olla had told her to avoid.

She picked up fistfuls of black dirt and filled her satchel with it carelessly. It was time to hurry back to the cabin as fast as she could, however tired or hungry or thirsty she may be. Before leaving, however, she looked up at the Womb and whispered a chant of *Warding*. The *life energy* in this area sang to her in a sweet and melodious tone. She had never ventured any further up the mountain, but she was sure that the *life energy* up there would feel overwhelming if not deafening to her. Quickly, she descended the dark slopes of the mountain into the woods, careful not to slide down the slick black rocks. As soon as her feet were on solid ground she dashed, against her best judgment. She knew her body had already taken quite the toll this day and would need rest soon, but Mother Olla needed her more.

An hour passed before she reached the Chleo once again. She knelt—almost collapsed, really—and filled her mouth with the icy water. She hadn't realized how thirsty she was. After several gulps, she wiped her mouth and caught her breath. That's when she felt it: a nearing *life energy*, one that slipped by her silent and unnoticed. Something moving darkly in the corner of her eye made her flinch. She noticed the matted tail just as it vanished behind a nearby bush. She was being stalked.

She stood slowly, eyes wide, and backed away. Her hand moved to her dagger, which she unsheathed carefully. The *greatwolf's* snout slowly materialized out of the bushes, followed by the rest of its large head. Its teeth were white, slaver foaming at the sides of its mouth. Its yellow eyes peered directly into hers, considering her every movement. Its ears flicked backward as it lunged for Adriel at a frightening speed. Adriel ran as fast as she could towards the thickest part of the forest. She dodged trees, zigzagging between them in hope of confusing the *greatwolf*, but the beast continued to chase her down, its paws hitting the ground silently as if it were a creature half its size. Adriel did her best to stay silent, but her panting grew into sobs of terror. She ran and ran, never looking back.

Suddenly, a piercing *shriek* filled the air, catching the young woman by surprise. Birds of all sort abandoned their perches, alarmed. Adriel's boot lost purchase on some wet leaves sending her thudding into the mud on her behind. The *shriek* continued for some time, high pitched and deafening. Adriel covered her ears to shield them from the terrible sound. After a few moments, the sound died: not just the *shriek*, but all sound in the woods came to a halt. The *greatwolf* was no longer chasing her. Adriel got to her feet, her right knee pulsating painfully. The leg of her pant was torn, revealing a bloody scrape underneath. She then turned her attention to the remarkable stillness around her. Even the wind seemed to have subsided.

Without a warning, the *thing* came crashing through the trees to land a few feet from her. The beast had four legs like those of a large wildcat, a body as thick and strong as that of a bear, and the face of an eagle. The dazzling silver feathers that covered its entirety caught her eye: in front of her stood a *melk*. In the *melk's* beak was the bloody ruined carcass of the *greatwolf* hanging as if weightless, its entrails forming a puddle on the ground below. The *melk's* eyes were black and wilder than anything she had ever seen. The beast's *life energy* felt as if it were trying to repel her, screaming at her to flee and fear.

Adriel felt like emptying herself. She watched frozen as the *melk* ate the *greatwolf* whole as easily as a spearhead snake ate an egg: a terrible sight. When the *greatwolf* disappeared down the silver beast's throat, the *melk* hunched over and ate the entrails, wasting no part of its kill. Adriel snapped back to reality as if she had come out from a deep dark dream. This was her moment to flee, right as the *melk's* attention was diverted from her.

She moved back a foot, then two, and suddenly the *melk's* head snapped up, and its eyes were right on her. She let out an involuntary yelp, and the *melk* matched it by *shrieking* its ear-splitting sound in her face. Adriel ran, and the beast followed. Zigzagging through the trees proved useless, the *melk* quickly slivering between the trees as if its bones were made of air. Every ache in Adriel's body was a faint memory, fear driving her deeper and deeper into the forest, the *melk* always mere seconds behind her. A dark thought crossed her mind: she was going to die. She was going to die, and so would Mother Olla and Yugo—although he was but an afterthought. They would die and it would all be her fault.

A gnarled root caught her ankle and sent her tumbling through the mud. She slid downhill like a ragdoll, hitting her head a few times and her back several. When she finally stopped her ragged fall, her vision was full of colorful speckles. Blindly, she felt her way through the mud and leaves for her satchel, which fell somewhere nearby. As her vision slowly filled in—the colorful speckles retreated to the corners of her eyes like a rainbow tunnel—she found her satchel, its contents spread about the muddy ravine she had fallen into. She frantically refilled it with the mushrooms and the black dirt, when a *shriek* filled the air yet again. Atop the ravine was the *melk*, looking down on her as if it were death itself.

Adriel shook in fear. She reached for her belt, for the small pouch tied next to her dagger. Mother Olla instructed her that an enchantress should always carry certain items and ingredients with her wherever she may be. She kept iron powder in her satchel, various golden needles safely stored in her hood pocket, and pink salt in a pouch at her belt. The *melk* walked up to her calmly: it knew its prey was too weak to run away. Adriel unfastened the small pouch and poured the coarse pink salt in a circle around her. She tossed the empty pouch aside, the wind sending it fluttering away, and bent to adjust the salt circle with her hands until it was closed and solid. Then she shut her eyes and chanted.

"*Adouns, melliat, endergo. Endergo, melliat ut heiro. Adouns, melliat, heiro endergo. Adouns, adouns...*"

She continued repeating the chant as she opened her eyes. The *melk* stood not even four feet from her. Adriel felt out of breath, her heart about to burst out of her throat. The creature slowly moved closer and closer, until its beak was directly in front of her face. Its smell, a mixture of fresh gore and decay, was only overpowered by the strange feeling of its energy. If the Womb of the World's *life energy* was a beautiful song, the *melk's* was a death knell. Adriel held her breath as the *melk* smelled her. And then, just when she thought her lungs would burst, the beast turned and retreated into the woods.

Adriel remained quiet until the silver-feathered creature had completely disappeared, and then she broke into sobs. For how long she cried, she couldn't say. When she eventually stopped, she looked up at the sky—the sun was setting, the heavy clouds reddening. Her body shook, still in shock, from fear, exhaustion, and pain. She struggled to collect her thoughts, not quite remembering what had set her out that day. Then thoughts of Mother Olla flooded back. It had been hours since she had left the old woman alone. If she didn't return to the cabin soon, the old woman would surely die—perhaps she had already.

Adriel realized her body would feel worse if she sat there, surrounded by the pink salt, so she forced herself to stand. Her bruised and bloody legs buckled. She took a few uncertain steps, pain shooting from her ankle to her neck. She had surely broken something. She broke a long sturdy branch from a nearby tree and used it to prop herself up.

She looked around, unsure of where she was exactly. She had never seen this ravine before, otherwise, she would have avoided the area. The surest thing was that the Chleo was east from here, so that's where she would head. Once she found the river, finding home would be easy.

As she proceeded through the woods in search of the river, Adriel thought back on the beast that had chased her down. A *melk*! In Albadone. It had been decades since the last sighting—so long that most people believed the creatures were nothing but a myth. Even Adriel had to admit she hadn't fully believed in the creatures until that morning when she found the feather. Mother Olla's books made mention of many other fantastical beasts that many considered nothing but legend: vampires, *djinns*, werewolves, and other monsters. How many of those were also real?

It didn't matter. What mattered was that *melk* were real and they were back in Albadone. The woodsfolk must be warned. Yolta, Brade, and their three children needed to be safe. But Mother Olla had to come first. Adriel grunted through the pain. It would be dark soon: she must hurry.

V.

THE COST

By the time Adriel reached the Chleo, the sun had started its final descent, still struggling to pierce through the darkening cloud cover. She crouched at the river and took a drink of cold water. Her heart told her there was no time to stop, but her mind knew better. A brief rest was warranted, especially after all she had gone through that day, from trekking to Chanter's Hill and back that morning, to running through the woods searching for ingredients and escaping from beasts. She tried to ignore the pain in her—she now was certain—broken foot. Forcing herself to walk on it would most likely injure her further, but that was the last thing on her mind at this moment. She washed the dirt and exhaustion from her face with the icy water and carried on.

As the forest darkened, fear overtook her determination once more. She saw *melk* in every bush and tree that surrounded her, leering, and waiting for a chance to pounce. She tried to be as quiet as possible, thanking the True One that the colorful leaves on the ground were soft and wet rather than dry and crunchy. Fearing the *melk*, she hadn't even considered the night's cold, which was descending upon the forest with uncaring ferocity. Just the past week one of the woodsfolk children had ventured out at night— for what reason, Adriel hadn't heard—and never returned. He was found the next morning, laying under a tree, skin blue and gray, crows picking at his body. In her haste to leave she had left her heavier hood at the cabin. Soon the cold would creep its icy fingers under her skin. No—she had to fix her eyes upon her goal and press on. Stopping in the cold Autumn nights of Albadone meant certain death.

A *shriek* pierced the air, too close for comfort. Adriel lowered her head, listening intently. The sound was close, but she couldn't feel the beast's *life energy* nearby; that was good. She moved onward. The cabin was a mile away, but the darkness made the forest harder to navigate—not even the moon was out to guide her tonight. A second *shriek* from another direction made her shiver. She couldn't be sure, but that sounded to her like another *melk* entirely. The implication of more than one *melk* in Albadone was unimaginable. She pressed on until she finally reached the clearing where her and Mother Olla's cabin stood. A final *shriek* startled her enough to make her slip and fall, her wooden support tumbling away from her. She turned towards the darkness of the woods, ghostly silhouettes observing her—or was she imagining them? She crawled through the mud until she reached the border of the pink salt circle she had laid out earlier.

A fire was lit inside, soft orange light giving the curtains an inviting glow. The effect of the curse must have passed or weakened for that to be possible. Adriel felt tears of joy readying themselves, but she put on a strong face. She wanted to look her best for her Mother. She rose, careful not to place too much weight on her broken foot. "Mother Olla! Is it safe to enter?" she called out.

There was no immediate response, which worried her. Then she heard it, faint and weak from inside. "Yes," the old woman whimpered.

Adriel crossed the salt circle and entered the cabin. Yugo was still on the floor exactly where he had been, however, it seemed Mother Olla had turned him onto his side. His eyes were still open in that death-like stare, drool pooling under his head. He seemed much older than she remembered, his hair thinning at his forehead and graying at his temples. Mother Olla lay on her cot. It seemed she had aged a decade or more in a single day. Her hair had whitened and shriveled up; all that remained were a few thin wisps. Her skeletal face was ragged and gaunt, her thin skin revealing the sharp cheekbones underneath. Cloudy gray eyes wandered the room aimlessly. In one bony hand was the *melk* feather, the other firmly holding onto the yellow runestone around her neck.

Adriel closed the door softly and made her way into the cabin. "Mother..." she said, a heavy lump at her throat.

"My child, you have returned," the old woman said weakly, smiling toothlessly.

"*Turtlewig* thorns, *whitecaps*, and black earth" Adriel listed, averting her eyes. Looking at the husk that sat where her Mother had been was heartbreaking. "I brought what you asked for."

"I knew you would... but it would seem this curse... has taken ahold of me... I am much too weak to perform this enchantment. I feel like... a shit that has been stepped on." The old woman smiled grotesquely. Even now, the woman's crass sense of humor remained.

Adriel couldn't help but laugh as tears warmed her cheeks. "Mother, I don't know if I am able."

"Don't worry, child. I will guide you every step of the way. You are a powerful enchantress... and you must believe... in yourself."

Adriel nodded, mostly to herself. "Anything for you, Mother. I will be your hands."

"That's my girl," the old woman said.

Adriel set her satchel on the workbench. Outside, a *shriek* disrupted the otherwise quiet night. Adriel quickly headed for the nearest window and drew the curtains aside. Outside was dark and impenetrable, but that sound felt so close.

"You mustn't worry, my child..." the old woman said. "The *melk* won't disturb us... Long ago, I have warded this cabin from their like..."

Adriel walked away from the window to the old woman. She propped her Mother's pillow up against the wall so that she could observe the workbench, assuring that she was comfortable. Mother Olla noticed the exhaustion in Adriel's face, as well as her limp and the gashes in her pants and hood. She lifted a weak hand to Adriel's face, rubbing dirt from her cheek. "My child... you are hurt."

"It's nothing, Mother," Adriel dismissed.

"I shall deal with it when I am better." She held Adriel's hand as tightly as she could, which wasn't very tight. Her hand felt feeble and thin, nothing like it had been. A memory of the warm woman holding her cold hand flashed across Adriel's mind. "Now hurry... for I am fading."

Adriel quickly moved to the workbench. She was so close to saving Mother Olla from this curse, she couldn't delay. From her satchel she produced the three ingredients, setting them all into a messy pile. The dirt had gotten everywhere—Adriel hoped it didn't matter.

"The enchantment is easy... even you could do it," Mother Olla said, followed by several muffled gasps. She was laughing. Adriel couldn't believe that even in this situation the woman had time to make jokes at her expense. "In a mortar, mash all three ingredients together... Release the essence, then sift..."

"What are the measurements?" Adriel asked as she retrieved the stone mortar and pestle from a shelf.

"Two thorns... two *whitecaps*... two spoons of earth..." the woman instructed. Her voice sounded dry and strained, weaker with each word.

Adriel did as she was told. Once the right amounts were placed in the mortar, she began mashing them quickly, but thoroughly, until a glistening muddy dark brown pulp had formed. "What comes next?"

"A chant... of *Binding*... twice..."

Adriel breathed deeply, then began, surely and steadily. "*Atoni, atoni, mel at frei*" As she chanted, she could hear the old woman's raspy voice softly joining in. "*Atoni, mel at frei ut endergo. Atoni it'atones ut maguyos.*" The unison of their voices filled her with memories of the old woman teaching her to chant when she was a young girl. This was the moment in which all her training, all she had learned, would serve her teacher. She knew that after tonight she would be a real enchantress.

After the two chants, Adriel opened her eyes. She lifted her hand to her face, realizing only then she had been crying. She looked over at the woman, awaiting further instruction. Mother Olla licked her dry lips. "This next part... is very important... you must drink two drops... no more, no less..."

Two drops? Had she misheard? "I'm not sure I understand?" Adriel asked.

"Two drops... drink it..." the old woman reiterated. *Why me?* As if she had read her mind, Mother Olla smiled. She slowly stood from the cot, her bones cracking like timber. Adriel quickly rushed to her and helped her remain standing. The old woman pointed at the workbench with a trembling hand, and Adriel walked her there slowly. Adriel tried to help her sit at the workbench, but the old woman refused, propping herself on the black stone. "You sit."

"But, Mother—"

"Sit, I say..." Adriel wasn't going to contradict the woman, especially not now, so she sat without complaint. Mother Olla placed the *melk* feather in Adriel's hair. "This poultice is... for you, my child... It is to awaken your true powers... I did this too... at your age... as did my Mother, and hers before her... without your true power, you may not rid me... of this curse."

Adriel looked down at the dark glistening concoction, considering. The old woman must have recognized this curse as unbreakable without some sort of external help. Adriel placed a lot of trust in the woman, but even she had her second thoughts.

"There is no time... I trust you, my child... Do you trust me...?"

I do. With no time to waste, Adriel retrieved a small steel pipette from the toolbox. She dipped one end of the pipette into the mortar, plugging the other end with her finger. She raised the pipette to her mouth and released exactly two drops of the dark concoction onto her tongue. The liquid tasted like bitter earth, but somehow it filled her with *life energy*; so much *life energy*, that she began to tremble involuntarily. As the liquid made its way down her throat, she felt the pain of her head, back, knee, and foot vanish without a trace. Warmth filled her from her head to her toes. She felt new. She felt powerful.

Then she felt the cold blade at her neck, saw the spray of warm blood pouring out. She choked, gasping for air. The old woman grabbed her by the hair and pulled her head back with unexpected force. Where had that strength come from? Adriel flailed about in a panic, her hands clawing at the chasm at her throat, struggling to keep herself whole.

Mother Olla shushed her gently, as a mother would with a crying daughter. "Soon there will be no pain, my child... Be glad... Your purpose is fulfilled." The old woman tugged on Adriel's hair until she fell onto the floor. She removed her necklace, the scar around her neck smiling, and unclasped the yellow runestone. Slowly, she knelt in front of the dying young woman, burying the runestone in her bloody gaping mouth. She forced Adriel's mouth shut and intoned a solemn chant.

"*Adournis, inieto ut ignotis mais eferve adurnis. Ameliatis ut adurnis.*"

It was a chant Adriel had never heard before. Why would the old woman keep this chant a secret? That being her final thought amused her.

As soon as the chant ended, the world went dark.

❦ ❦ ❦ ❦

Mother Olla woke up choking on blood and the stone in her mouth. She spat the runestone out in her right hand and held her neck shut with the other. She wiped the blood off the runestone, revealing that the etching of *Binding* had been shattered. The *Transference* ritual was successful. Her old withering body lay on the ground, dead and cold. She stood and sat at the workbench, blood still gushing from the wound at her neck. She quickly picked out a golden needle from the toolbox and some thread and placed a small looking glass in front of her. Mother Olla began sewing her neck shut. The *life energy* coursing through her made the pain appear distant, as if it were happening to someone else.

How many times had she done this? She couldn't recall. Many—too many perhaps. It was what needed to be done. She had had many names through the centuries, too many to remember. Only one stood out: her first, the one she had been born with. But the name had been cursed and she dared not speak it, lest she bring to a halt this never-ending cycle of rebirth she had devised for herself. Adriel had been one of her brightest students, with one of the most powerful connections to nature and *life energy*. That power would now be hers, but she couldn't help the loss she felt for the girl.

No! You mustn't feel for her. She served her purpose. She is gone forever now. Only you remain. You, forever. The work of an enchantress was never over.

When she was done with mending her wound, she headed outside. She couldn't feel the cold at all, *life energy* warming every fiber of her being like a furnace—in fact, she almost felt too warm, like a walking bonfire. It took several hours to build the pyre the way it was meant to be, with the right measurements and the right sort of wood—she had told Adriel to keep buying that wood from neighboring woodsfolk but told her to never burn it. *Stop thinking about the girl, you weak old shit! She is gone forever!*

It was morning when she placed her old body atop the pyre—the yellow runestone placed on its chest—and lit it with a flint. She chanted all seven chants and danced naked around the fire until it had burned out and the sky was light blue with first light. She collected the ashes of her former body in a small leather pouch sealed with blessed twine—those ashes would serve her in the future—and picked the spent runestone from among the embers: it had turned gray and rough as a regular stone. She placed the spent runestone at the very end of the *spyrale*. Starting that spiral-shaped display was nothing but a faint memory, as were the names of every Mother she had been. Why she had shaped it that way, she could barely remember. It must have had a meaning. Adriel had always asked about it—*Enough with the girl!*

Still naked, she washed the brown dry blood from her body and neck, then from the cabin floors, and threw her bloody clothes into the fireplace. From under her cot, she pulled out fresh linens, the ones she kept clean and ready for this exact moment. Adriel had often asked her about those, but she had never given the girl a straight answer. *Damn that girl's curiosity.* It had been what she had admired most about her. She always asked questions and never took anything for truth until she knew it for a fact.

Mother Olla felt the disgust build up in her belly. She wanted to throw up or die or both, but it was too late. This was the path she had chosen to take. There was no turning back.

She diverted her attention to her dresser—the one gifted to her decades ago by a lover who had been a very rich Maegoldian merchant. She opened a drawer, revealing runestones of every color in the rainbow. She pulled out a yellow one with the cross-shaped seal of *Binding*, clasped it to her necklace, and donned it around her neck, covering her fresh stitches. Then she looked over at the young knight, still laying on the floor. Yugo had aged considerably due to the curse, now appearing as a man of middle age. She knew she could fix him, but it would take time and resources. She rummaged among her vials, picking out one filled with a coarse white powder. She placed the vial near Yugo's nose, only then uncorking it. Yugo's head shot up suddenly, gasping as if he had been submerged this entire time. Mother Olla immediately recorked the vial and placed it aside. She held the man's face in her gentle young hands, his eyes wide and fearful.

"It's all right," she reassured. "You're all right."

It took a few moments for the young knight to calm down. He clenched his eyes—no doubt dry as anything from being open this entire time—and took in a few deep breaths. "What happened?" he asked, his voice gravely and spent.

"The rune you gave us... It contained an evil curse. It aged you considerably, but I can fix you." Yugo lifted his hand to touch hers. At the sight of the wrinkles and blotches covering his aged hand, his eyes widened once again. "You have to trust me."

Yugo nodded. His dry red eyes watered uncontrollably. "What about the old woman? Where is she?"

It took her a few moments for her to register the question. She frowned, feigning sadness. "She... she didn't make it."

Yugo's eyes lowered, his mouth agape in disbelief. "I'm so sorry. If it weren't for me none of this would have ever happened."

"Her body was old and frail," she interrupted. "The curse was much too strong for her body to bear. But her soul is strong and will live on. That's the truth that we live by as children of the True One." That seemed to put him somewhat at ease. She wiped a tear from his cheek with a kind finger. "You need to eat something, child; get you back to health so I can restore you to your proper self. Then you can return to your questing and knighting."

"Thank you, Adriel," Yugo said.

She smiled. "You may call me Mother."

WINTER:
A FATHER

VI.

A Drunk

The quiet of the forest of Albadone was interrupted by the heavy sloshing of boots through the moonlit snow. After the cold Autumn they just had, it was a common belief that the Winter would be milder. This hadn't been the case.

Handel could barely feel the bite of the cold thanks to the warm wine coat he was cocooned within as he trudged unsteadily forward. Most workdays ended this way—him stumbling through the woods on his way home, drunk. His work hours were long, and the labor was arduous. Handel hated every minute of it. The worst part, though, was that Brade, the foreman, hadn't been at all clear about what they were building. At first, he had said they were digging a well, then when they found no water, he changed his mind and told them they were building a mill. When anyone asked, all he would say was *"either get the job done or leave my worksite."* Handel had long since stopped asking, but the frustration remained. Sure, he was being paid, but paid to do what exactly? Not knowing made him feel like such a fool. If it weren't for the fact that Brade's wife, Yolta, and Myr—his wife—were childhood friends, he would have punched that smug woodsman long ago.

Handel found solace in drinking. It was the only thing he had control over. All he had to look forward to in his day to day life was an ill-defined work that gave him no pleasure, a nagging wife, and a sick daughter. *What did I do to deserve all this?* he thought, his eyes straining to keep the path ahead of him from swimming and sloshing like the wine souring in his stomach. He was meant for greater things—or so he told himself. He had an adventurous spirit in his youth when he was lean, handsome, and had hair. Why did he even marry in the first place? It was what he ought to do, he had thought. *Damn that woman.* If it weren't for her, he'd be far from this forsaken forest by now, perhaps in Fendleton, or as far as Sol Forne—he heard they had good wine there. And hell, he could use another drink about now.

He shook his head. The woman always nagged at him whenever he spent all their pieces on booze. But how else was he supposed to survive the cold walk home in the dead of night? That was it. If he didn't drink himself beet-red every night, he would die from the cold. Surely, the woman should understand that—unless perhaps she meant him dead. Then she wouldn't have to work and could marry someone rich, with hair, who could care for their sick girl; then they would have a bigger home, with real beds and the garden she had always wanted.

Handel hunched over and emptied his stomach under a tree. He wiped the sick from his mouth and stumbled onwards, towards town. The lanterns were still lit, thank the gods! The last time he returned to town this late they had already been put out, and he had been left to feel his way home through the inky blackness. Pevine was a small town on the southern outskirts of the forest. The next town over, to the northwest, was that shithole Lorne, then Vizen—the capital—to the west. He had always wanted to visit the capital, with its paved roads and high towers, but now that wish aggravated him—made him feel small. He couldn't tell if he resented never achieving those dreams or himself for having ever had them.

He tried to be quiet—Myr hated when a neighbor caught him walking home drunk—but that damn slurry of snow and mud squelched loudly under his feet despite his every drunken effort at grace. His house was at the very back of the village—where the outcasts lived. He knew everyone in town avoided his family and looked down on them. Myr told him it was all in his head, but what did she know? She didn't have to deal with the looks the other men gave him at the worksite. He knew they thought him a deadweight—a drunken idiot who couldn't even afford medicine for his dying daughter.

Damn them! His fist collided with the wall of a nearby building—once, then twice. He felt warm blood fill his hand; dull pain and regret—a familiar feeling. An old man stuck his head out of a window. "Hey!" he yelled in a groggy voice. "Get your arse home, Handel, you drunk bastard!"

"Shut your mouth," Handel slurred, holding his throbbing hand tightly. That had to have been Yelvin. Or perhaps Peter. He wasn't certain which house he had punched. *Fuck him, either way.*

"Bah!" The old man waved him off and disappeared into the home.

"Yeah, you better run," Handel yelled out. Around him, windows filled with his neighbors, watching him—with judging eyes. Hot embarrassment colored his face. He lowered his gaze, and moved onwards, towards his home at the edge of the village. *Criticism comes easily to those who are comfortable*, he brooded.

The house was decently sized but in urgent disrepair. While it had two bedrooms, only one was usable in the Winter—as the other was much too drafty and cold to be slept in—so he and Myr slept on mats in the living area. The house had belonged to Myr's uncle, who died in his sleep of a chest cold—no surprise there. *Lucky bastard.* He and Myr were newlyweds at the time, still living with her mother in the woods. The house should have been a fresh start for them, but instead, it had been the beginning of all their troubles. Gray smoke rising from the chimney indicated a fire was burning—no doubt Myr had forgotten to put it out again. He walked up to the old rotting door and missed the doorknob by several inches. When he finally caught it, he opened the door, careful to not make a sound. Slowly he entered the warm home.

"Where have you been?" The coldness of Myr's voice was enough to dissipate the warmth of the fireplace.

Handel sighed heavily. As always, his wife had stayed up to wait for him—no, to *catch* him—returning home late and drunk. She stood at the other side of the room still wearing her work clothes, her dark curls tossed in a messy bun. She seemed tired but focused. Her arms were crossed below her breasts: a bad sign.

"I was at work," he replied, doing his best to enunciate. He removed his sludge-covered boots and dropped them carelessly onto the floor.

"Work," she repeated, tasting the word. Her eyes were on the boots, but she remained focused on the matter at hand—one admonishment at a time.

"That's what I said. *Work.*" Handel hated this. Why couldn't the woman just let him be? His eyes burned and his head was swimming—the room wobbled to and fro as if he stood on the back of a mule cart. He removed his heavy Winter cloak and dropped it on the ground over the boots. He knew that wasn't where it belonged, but he felt a sort of satisfaction in irritating Myr.

"You're drunk," she stated, very matter-of-factly.

"And?"

"What do you mean *and?*"

Handel had had enough of this. He dismissed her with a wave and headed to where an iron basin filled with water sat on a stool by the window. Handel filled his large hands with the lukewarm water and splashed it on his face.

"Ellie kept asking where you were," Myr said. The woman always used their daughter as a means to hurt him. "Even I started to wonder after a while."

"I'll go see her in a moment," he said between rinses.

"No, you won't," Myr admonished. "She's asleep."

Handel picked up a dry cloth from a pile on the floor and wiped his face. "You can't tell me what to do." He said it almost without slurring.

"You're drunk."

"And you're a bitch."

"Papa?"

Handel and Myr turned almost in unison towards the far room. Ellie leaned unsteadily against the doorframe. The little girl was almost six years old, but she appeared smaller and much younger due to the illness that had kept her bound to her bed for the past few years. She spent most of her time at home resting, only managing to stand and walk outside a couple of times a week—although recently she was weakening by the day, and so a couple of times a week had turned into a couple of times a month. Nevertheless, the girl stood now, a large smile on her gaunt face. She ran, or rather, tottered, as fast as she was able into the living area, collapsing right in front of Handel. The man caught her before she hit the floor, then filled her thinning auburn hair with kisses.

"What are you doing out here, Ellie?" Handel asked, the surprise sobering him somewhat.

"I heard your voice and I wanted to see you." The girl smiled. "I missed you, Papa."

Handel hugged her tightly. "I missed you too," he said, shooting a pointed glance at Myr, who stared at him as if the spit in her mouth was curdling. Ellie began to cough dryly. "Come on," Handel said. "Let's get you back to bed."

He picked Ellie up as if she were air and took her to her bedroom. Myr didn't follow them in. He set the girl onto her bed—a cot stuffed with hay and feathers—and pulled the covers over her tightly. Her candle was still lit, filling the small room with a fluttering orange glow. The girl's hot breath came out as a shallow wheeze.

She should not have tried to run as she had—but he appreciated her doing so. His and Myr's argument would have devolved into screaming. They all had lately. He kissed the girl on her damp, warm, forehead. "Have a good night, Ellie," he said.

"Can you tell me a story first, Papa?" she asked sweetly.

"I don't think that's such a good idea." His head was still hot and heavy. A slight ache at the back of his eyes warned him it was time to go to sleep soon.

"Please, Papa? Just one," she implored, holding onto his wide forearm.

He resigned with a sigh. "What sort of story do you want to hear?"

"Tell me about the tree."

"The tree? What tree, Ellie?" He had a suspicion of what she meant. He prayed he was wrong.

"The wishing tree," she said. Her smile was the sole thing that didn't betray the weakness of her condition. *Gods!* Why was she bringing this up now? "Momma said that when she was little, she walked into the woods and found a wishing tree." There it was—that damn woman was filling her head with this nonsense again.

"Your mother shouldn't be telling you those stories," he interrupted rather brusquely. The girl's smile disappeared almost instantly. "If you want, I can tell you about the time I built a cabin with my brother—"

"—and then it flooded," she finished. "I heard that one a million times. Is it true that the wishing tree helps people with their problems?"

The headache became a shard of glass poking at his skull. *Anything but this insanity.* "The wishing tree gives people something. Whether it helps or not," he trailed off, "depends on who is telling the story."

"Momma says you hate the tree," she spat the words out between coughs—it really was getting worse each day.

A cold breeze made the candle flicker. Handel turned to the window and closed it. "Your mother should have closed this. It's too cold for you."

"I asked her to keep it open," she grinned meekly, "so I could see you arrive."

Handel's back stiffened. Had she seen him stumble drunkenly through the night like a monster? "You must rest now, Ellie. Us both. I have a long day ahead of me tomorrow."

Her disappointment would have broken his heart had he not been harboring hotly pulsating anger. Ellie sighed and closed her eyes as if to shut him out. He leaned in and kissed her cheek. Another coughing fit suddenly took hold of her, making her body spasm uncontrollably. Handel held her gently, putting his arm in front of her face. When the fit finally ended, Ellie rolled over and was immediately asleep, exhausted—those fits drained her of energy. Speckles of blood covered the sleeve of Handel's shirt where the girl had coughed. Why couldn't he just make her pain go away? He blew out the candle and left the room quietly.

Handel entered the living area and sat on the wobbly wooden chair, which groaned under his weight. Myr sat on her sleeping mat, drinking what smelled like wine out of a clay mug. It was far, but the smell was enough to make him gag.

"I can't believe you told the girl about the wishing tree," he said, holding his heavy head in his hands. Myr chuckled softly to herself. "I won't take part in this sort of... magical woodsfolk nonsense." Truly, he still didn't understand much of woodsfolk culture, their strange beliefs, legends, and their 'True One'. As of late, some were even saying that *melk* had returned to the woods.

He was originally from Rondhill, a large city of commerce to the east—a crossroads of *real* culture and enterprise. He had moved to the forest of Albadone to find work. In Rondhill, anyone that claimed *melk* or wishing trees were real would have been sent straight to the chemists for prodding.

Myr took a sip of her wine, her face a mask of calm. "It's not nonsense," she said levelly. "All woodsfolk know about the wishing trees, and you know very well I had my own," she paused, "experience with one. I asked a wishing tree to save my mother from my father's daily physical tortures—"

"—and you pulled out a knife," Handel interrupted dismissively. Myr calmly raised the cup to her mouth. He felt bad for the way he had said it, but she was the one who brought it up. He never outright said he didn't believe her, but the implication was always in the air. "Nothing in this world is given for free."

"I was only twelve years old. Do you think what happened next didn't come at a cost?" Her voice was firm, but there was pain behind her eyes. He remembered the first time she had told him that story: she had sobbed it into his shoulder as he held her and smoothed her hair. Why couldn't he bring himself to even look at her now? "One cannot ask a wishing tree for help more than once in their lifetime without paying an ultimate cost," she continued, undeterred. "So even though I would love nothing more than to venture into the woods, search for a wishing tree, and ask it to save our precious girl..." her voice cracked softly. "I can't."

Silence fell between them. Handel wanted to scream, to break something—to flee—but he couldn't even bring himself to move. Powerless. As always. He focused his attention on the pain that still pulsed in his knuckles, hoping that it would get worse, that it could be the only thing he felt. Myr stood to her feet. She grabbed his injured hand and wiped the blood away with a clean cloth, gently and lovingly. He wanted her to hit him, to make him hurt more. Then his feelings towards her would be justified.

"You know we can't afford to take her to a chemist or healer or even buy the medicine she needs," Myr said. *Will this woman not yield?* Handel pulled his hand away from her and stood up. He was several heads taller than her—and than most people. Why did he feel so small?

"I have a long day tomorrow," he said, heading for his mat. As he lay there, his awareness shrinking down around the pain in his hand, he could sense Myr's quiet sobs. She never wanted him to hear her cry—but he always did.

VII.

A Wasted Workday

The bustling worksite sat in a large circular clearing that had been carved into the dense forest. At the center of the circle stood a tall wooden structure—the *bore*, Brade called it. Metal pipes ran down its innards like a spine to enter a dark wide cavern underneath. It was at least three times wider than the widest well in Albadone. Inside the pit, miners dug into the black earth. Buckets of it were pulled out of the hole through a system of ropes and pulleys. Outside the inner circle of workers were the smiths, fashioning more hollow steel pipes so that the *bore* might reach further into the ground, and barrel makers—Brade hadn't been clear what those large barrels were for at all. At the furthest edges of the worksite were the woodworkers and lumbermen, cutting down trees and fashioning them into planks.

Handel sat at his workbench at the very far edge of the worksite, eyes sunken and skin pale. A lumberman split a log a few feet behind him that might as well have been his head. He felt like death and looked like it too. One of his fellow workers—Ian was his name if Handel recalled correctly—stared at him strangely. Handel was about to ask him what his problem was when he looked down at his work: he had been sanding a plank in the same spot over and over until it had grown thinner than the rest. Ian smirked and returned his attention to his own work. Handel wanted to break the plank over that smirking bastard's face, if only his head hadn't been trying to swallow his body whole. He stood and tossed the plank onto the nearby pile of scrap wood.

He wasn't a woodworker by trade, rather by necessity. As a young man in Rondhill, he was an apprentice innkeeper at one of the finest inns in the region—or so his master boasted—*the Lonesome Squire*. Master Ellos was already old and frail when Handel met him. One of Ello's sons had forsaken his father's wishes to open an inn in Vizen. His only other son, Todden, had died years earlier in the siege of Redrock—Handel knew the boy's name because Master Ellos had called him by it numerous times in error. After three years of apprenticeship, the old man had promised him that the *Squire* would be his upon his death. However, when that day came, but six months later, Master Ellos' son returned from Vizen and seized the inn. *"I don't see in writing where it says it's yours,"* the man said. *"If you don't leave now, I'll have the guard come and flog you all the way to Vizen."* Handel had no choice. He left his livelihood and the place he had called home to become a woodworker in the forest.

The lunch bell rang. *Thank the gods.* Handel stood from his workbench feeling twice his weight. If he couldn't go about his day without feeling ill, he would have to cover the hangover with more wine. *Curing overindulgence with drink is like putting out a fire with leaves*—one of the stupid woodsfolk sayings popped into his head; where had he heard that one? He couldn't recall. A line had already formed in front of the mess table. By the smell of it, they were serving beef stew again—they called it beef stew but the broth itself contained merely the bones and a faint smell of meat. It was a fine stew that succeeded in filling and warming up the workers, but what Handel cared about now were the wineskins that were given out to each of them—drinking on the job was a bit of woodsfolk culture he could approve of. Nothing kept you warmer on a hard Winter's day than wine.

Handel tapped impatiently with his boot onto the wet ground as he stood in line. Finally, when it was his turn, Thelmo—a hardy man that appeared better suited for fighting than cooking—poured a bowl of stew and handed it to him. "Next," he said, to Handel's surprise.

"And the wine?" Handel asked.

"None today," was all he said, dismissing him with a nod.

Heat rose in Handel's cheeks, his head pulsing like a tick on a dog. "What do you mean none today?"

"It's Winter and the price of wine has increased," Thelmo calmly explained. "We can now afford it only once a week. This was explained to you at the meet three days ago. Didn't you pay attention?" It just so happened, he had not. At the start of each workweek, Brade, the foreman, stood atop a stool and addressed all the workers, keeping them updated with their progress and the goals for the month. Handel had stopped paying attention to those speeches several months earlier. The authority with which the short man spoke irritated him. "Next," the cook reiterated, pouring a bowl of stew for the next man in line.

Handel left his bowl by the pot and stormed off. His vision darkened at the edges, as he paced aimlessly about the worksite. A group of men was loading sacks on top of a mule cart by the tree line. The cart transported minerals, roots, earth, and what-have-you to town to sell to merchants and apothecaries. *That's it!* He would hitch a ride on the back of the cart to town, grab a drink of wine—or two—and return before the lunch hour ended. He approached the cart, stopping in front of the group of men. His head spun from the exertion—perhaps he should have taken that bowl of stew, but it was too late for that now.

The workers turned to face him with inquisitive looks. "If it isn't Handel," the one named Tir said, folding his arms, a grin stretching his pox-scarred face. "What can we do for you?"

Handel ignored him and turned his attention to the cart driver, a stocky woodsman with three chins. "Please sir, could I ride on the back of the cart? I have urgent matters to attend to in town."

"Urgent matters?" Tir laughed. "If by urgent matters you mean getting urgently piss-faced drunk, then by all means." The other men laughed. Handel kept his eyes on the driver, although a flush of anger rose on the back of his neck, coloring his ears hotly—he prayed they did not see it.

"I don't take passengers," the driver said flatly, then turned to secure a sack on the back of the cart.

"Please, sir, I—"

"Allow me to make a suggestion," Tir interrupted. "Perhaps if you piss in a cup and drink it, you might be able to get drunk off of that." The men laughed loudly—even the driver cracked a smile. "We all saw how drunk you were last night." Tir stumbled about, doing an exaggerated impersonation of Handel.

Anger found Handel's fist smashing against Tir's jaw. The man collapsed unconsciously onto the muddy ground. The rest of the men stared at him in disbelief; in fact, he wasn't sure himself what he had just done. A blonde-haired man shoved him on the shoulder, but Handel didn't budge—stubby woodsfolk arms could only do so much against somebody his size; a brawl between woodsfolk and townsfolk usually ended with several broken noses on the side of the woodsfolk.

"Enough!" a voice barked from a few feet away. Brade paced towards them, his mood as dark as his beard. He was short, even by woodsfolk standards, but he had a strong, broad, upper body, wide forearms, and a direct manner of speech that commanded respect. "What's going on here?" he asked—no, demanded.

"Handel punched Tir," the blonde man said, pointing at him.

Brade investigated Handel, eyes landing almost instantly on his bloody knuckles—the punch had reopened yesterday's wound. "I want you gone from the worksite for the day," he commanded. "You will be compensated for the hours you have worked. Return tomorrow with a better mood and a cooler head." And with that, Brade turned his attention to the downed man, putting calloused fingers at his nose to check for breathing. "He'll be all right. Take him somewhere where he can rest until he's able to stand." The men picked Tir up by his shoulders and legs and took him away. When Brade noticed Handel still standing there, his face creased with irritation—much like that of a parent finding out a child has disobeyed them. "Didn't I dismiss you?"

Handel's eyes dropped.

"And take care of yourself, Handel. Your family needs you."

What did Brade know about what his family needed? The man had no right to bring them up. Handel could feel eyes all over him as he walked out of the worksite and into the woods. This day had gone from bad to worse in moments. All he wanted was a damn drink of wine; was that so much to ask? Gods knew he deserved it. He had given up so much to have so little. He would have a drink of wine today if it was the last thing he did. These damn woodsfolk all knew each other, and the gossip of Handel getting kicked off the worksite would no doubt find its way to Myr by sundown. If he had to survive her nagging, he would do it with a belly full of drink. He made his way to town, on a quest.

The afternoon market was in full swing when he arrived an hour later. Crowds of townsfolk, woodsfolk, and even some folk from Vizen it seemed, hustled about, buying, selling, and trading all sorts of wares, from spices to enchanted items, and even furniture and livestock. Pevine was situated centrally between the forest of Albadone and the cities to the west, making it the perfect center of commerce between the two worlds. Myr tended a stall at the morning market, while Ellie was still fast asleep, but would have made her way home by now, so this was the perfect time of day for Handel to be there. In his current condition, however, the sights and smells exhausted him. The endless chatter of shoppers was like hornets droning. His stomach was attempting to eat itself, and his head was jumping up and down on his shoulders. He passed a group of young men and women crowded in front of the work board and made his way towards *The Rat's Nest*—a humble tavern that visitors from out of town tended to avoid.

Inside, the tavern was warm and quiet. The only patrons were two men silently smoking pipes, their blue smoke lifting into the air and snaking through the small place—its sweet smell almost made Handel keel over. He quickly headed for Alanda, the lovely young barmaid. Her dark red hair was collected casually into a bun atop her head. In her arms she held a sleeping newborn baby—Handel had no idea she had been with child, but that just went to show how much he paid attention to his neighbors. He bought himself a mug of wine and a bowl of seedberries to keep his stomach from souring. The cook at the worksite was right: the price of wine had almost doubled. But he didn't care.

He lifted the mug to his mouth and poured the wine down in three steady gulps. Already, he felt better—his headache replaced by warm wool. Handel reached into his coat for more pieces, but he didn't have enough for another round. Then he remembered Myr had been drinking wine from a mug the night before—how hypocritical of her to judge his drinking. No doubt she spent her days getting drunk herself, instead of working and watching the girl—like she was supposed to. He wasn't looking forward to the nagging he would receive for not being at work, but he needed another drink sooner rather than later—he would have to come up with a convincing story.

He stepped out of the dark tavern and into the blinding Winter afternoon to make his way home. The crowds were still thick—thicker even—and louder than ever. As he navigated through the sea of people, he found himself stuck shoulder to shoulder in a wall of men. Sick began to build in his stomach again, the warm wool releasing its comforting hold over him. He pushed his way through the crowd until he turned into the alleyway between the butcher shop and the community oven—it was the long way home, but at least it was clear of the crowd. It was empty, in fact, except for a hooded woman, walking out of the alleyway in Handel's direction, and a large townsman in front of him. The woman, who seemed to be going through several old letters, distractedly bumped into the townsman as they passed.

"Watch where you're going, girl!" the man said venomously. The woman gave the townsman a cursory glance, then made her way past Handel before vanishing into the river of townsfolk he had just escaped. The townsman turned to him and said, "These woodsfolk whores don't give us the respect we deserve." He waited for a moment for Handel to agree, then moved along. Handel continued behind the man until he saw a small piece of brown paper on the ground. He picked it up before the wind could catch it. It was a stained envelope that read: *To Mother Olla*.

Shit. Everyone in Pevine knew who Mother Olla was—the old enchantress that lived in the forest. Woodsfolk revered the woman as some kind of living deity. Enchanting and runesmithing were respected skills, but they were only that: anyone could learn them, just like woodworking. Handel wanted nothing to do with the woman, nor any other woodsfolk legends or tales for that matter. He wanted to leave the letter where he found it. *A fool doesn't aid a friend, but only a dead man doesn't aid an enchantress*—another one of those woodsfolk sayings; *they really did have a saying for all damn things*. Handel held onto the letter for a few moments, then made his decision, regretting it almost instantly. He turned and headed out of the alleyway and into the crowd, his eyes scanning for the woman's cloaked shape.

As he shuffled slowly forward, his irritation made way for anger. Some of these piss-headed people simply would not move out of his way. He nearly barked at an unmoving old woman sniffing yellow spice blends from a large sack, until he saw she was accompanied by an armed retinue. When he finally did manage to pass the old woman—who no doubt would be sprouting roots at her feet any moment now—he made his way to where the raw runestones and trinkets were sold. If this hooded woman worked for the old enchantress, this would be a great place to find her. He wanted to get this over with as soon as possible. The runestone merchant was already packing up his wares by the time he arrived. There was no trace of the woman.

"You, there," he asked the merchant, trying to get his attention. The man was of Handel's age, dark-skinned and bald. His arms were covered in swirling drawings that reminded him of a painting of the ocean waves that Master Ellos had hung in the common room of *the Squire*. "Have you seen a hooded woman around here?"

"I've seen many hooded women," he said in an accent Handel didn't recognize. "It is cold here in Winter."

"Her hood is dark." Handel realized he hadn't gotten a good look at any of the woman's features. "She was carrying letters." The merchant looked at the letter in Handel's hand, his inquisitive expression giving way to confusion. "She dropped this on the ground. I want to return it to her."

The man flashed a smile—his teeth were the whitest and straightest Handel had ever seen. "Mother Adriel is who you're searching for. A fine young enchantress. After coming to me, she usually goes to the smith to pick up tools. Maybe ask there."

Handel headed over to the smith's stall, which was helpfully close by, without sparing the man another word. Gerron was the smith's name, a broadly muscled man who provided ax heads for the worksite. After asking about the *bore*, and talking at length about a new type of steel that had been crafted with the minerals provided by Brade—Gerron always did have a way of not letting anyone have a word in—Handel managed to ask about the hooded enchantress.

Thankfully, it seemed she hadn't stopped by there yet, but she would soon, to receive a golden hammer she had ordered. *A golden hammer? With that much gold, I could buy all the wine in Pevine.* The thought quickly festered in his head. *No. With that much gold, I could buy Ellie the medicine she needs. What's wrong with me?*

Moments went by, filled by Gerron's incessant yapping—didn't the man have work to do? Handel's head felt hotter than the forge fires. He could have dropped off the letter with the blacksmith and gone home, but something told him he had to hand it directly to the woman. Finally, she arrived. The dark hood that covered her head cast a straight shadow across her face, making it hard to see her clearly. Her only visible features were full lips, and a necklace holding a shiny yellow runestone.

"Do you have something for me?"

It took Handel a few moments to realize he was being addressed. The woman pointed at the letter in his hand. "Oh, yes," he said absentmindedly. "Here you are, Mother." The word felt clumsy and forced in his mouth, but it was the proper way to refer to an enchantress.

The woman took the letter in her gloved hand and stored it in a satchel. "I can be so distracted at times. Thank you…"

"Handel."

"Thank you, Handel." She smiled—had she not been an enchantress, this would have been pleasant even. "You might not know it, but you saved me much gripe. How can I ever repay you?"

"It's nothing really," he said. All he wanted at that moment was to go home and drink the day away.

"You must have heard who I am, and what I do," she said, that strange smile still on her lips. She had a way of speaking that didn't sound quite natural coming out of that mouth. "If there's something you need, please don't hesitate to ask. If it's within my power, I'll be happy to oblige."

Suddenly, Handel's mind was flooded by thoughts of his daughter. This woman was an enchantress, not a healer; but perhaps there was something she could do—*No! Asking an enchantress for help opens the door to more woodsfolk nonsense. Next thing, you'll be praying to their True One.*

The young woman stared at him, her eyes flashing like a cat's underneath that hood. Her smile widened. "There is something, isn't there?"

It was as if his mouth had been sewed shut. Why was it so hard for him to ask for help? When was the last time he had been able to rely on someone? Had there been anyone since Master Ellos died?

Ellie needs me.

"My daughter. She's... she's dying..." he said, forcing the words out between his teeth. "My wife wants me to go find a... a *wishing tree*." He spat the final words as if they were a curse. "She wants me to ask it to heal her. I know, it's silly."

Mother Adriel moved closer to him, lifting his chin with a gentle hand. She was about as tall as his chest, but the simple gesture gave her stature. "A father wanting to save his daughter. What's so silly about that? I'm no healer, so I can't help your daughter." *Of course, she can't, you fool.* "However, there is a way I can help you find a wishing tree. Those trees are very rare nowadays, most of them having been killed by you townsfolk." It wasn't an accusation, just a simple fact.

"I want nothing to do with wishing trees," he said. He knew he was contradicting himself. "Some things in this world are better left alone."

"Wise words," she said, letting go of his chin. "But words are just that; they do nothing to heal your daughter." She reached into her satchel and pulled out a dull pearl-colored runestone. "This is a runestone of *Guidance*," she explained. "I crafted it myself. As long as you have a clear vision in your mind, this will help you find what you seek."

"I cannot accept," said Handel. He didn't *want* anything to do with this. *But Ellie...*

Mother Adriel huffed and shook her head, as one might do with an unruly child. She grabbed Handel's hand and dropped the stone in it, wrapping his fingers around it. "Has no one ever told you it's bad luck to refuse a gift from an enchantress, child?"

Handel held the stone in his hand, contemplating it, feeling its weight.

"May the True One guide you in your quest, and may you find what you seek." With that, she turned to the blacksmith to collect her order.

VIII.

The Wishing Tree

Handel never got around to having that drink of wine. Once home, Myr lobbed him with questions about what had happened at the worksite, and what he was doing home so early. Thankful that she hadn't already heard, he didn't fight. All he said was "I wasn't feeling well, so I asked to go home." By the grace of the gods, somehow, she believed him—it must have been his level tone. In truth, his mind was elsewhere. He kept his hand in his pocket, running his fingers across the smooth surface of the pearl-colored runestone.

Am I really considering following through with this insane quest? Seeking a wishing tree with a runestone! Even thinking about it filled him with such conflicting emotions—it went against everything he believed. But then there was Ellie. The last time they had taken her to a chemist, the previous Spring, he had told them that she would not survive past Winter. Her cough would grow worse until, eventually, she would stop breathing. Any day could be her last. Surely, it couldn't be so simple as asking a tree for a wish. Handel couldn't wrap his head around it. All his life he had struggled. He had struggled in vain at the inn; now he struggled for the little he did have. To live was to struggle.

Myr served him a bowl of boiled potatoes and purple carrots. He was more sick than hungry, but he forced himself to eat nonetheless. It was good to have something warm filling his belly. All of a sudden, he felt sleep encroaching on him as if a warm blanket had wrapped itself around his shoulders. He lay on his cot as exhaustion took hold of him and fell asleep almost instantly. When he woke up, later that evening, Ellie lay asleep next to him, her softly shivering body wrapped around his. He remained still so as not to wake her. Her eyes fluttered as she dreamed, her breath coming out dry and shallow. He kissed her head, wishing her the best of dreams.

"She wanted to see you," Myr whispered. Handel turned his head to face her. She sat on her mat a few feet away, her legs crossed as she mended a neighbor's cloak, another way of gaining extra pieces for the household. "She was so excited when I told her you were home early. I brought her over. I hope you don't mind."

"I don't mind," he said, running his fingers through her damp hair. For a few moments, the only sound in the house was the crackling of the fire. Handel reached into his pocket: the runestone sat there solidly, a reminder. A knot formed in his throat. Ellie's wheezing breath gently tickled his beard—he had so much to lose. "Myr," he called out silently, hoping she had both heard him and not. It suddenly occurred to Handel that it had been a long time since he had said her name aloud.

"Yes, Handel?" she asked, awaiting a reply.

He wished she hadn't heard. "Nothing," he replied.

He barely slept that night, his mind racing. After the cloak was fully mended and she had washed up, Myr eventually went to bed. He heard her disrobe and fit herself under the blankets. At that moment he wanted to hold her, to tell her that he had decided to try the wishing tree. But the words felt trapped within him and her body felt much farther away than the few feet that actually separated them. He lay there, motionless, sleeping on and off until the curtains glowed purple in the first light. He gently rolled Ellie aside and got out of his mat. He pulled the wool blankets tightly over the girl and kissed her forehead, before donning his work clothes, his heavy Winter cloak—the one Myr had made him before Ellie was even born—and his boots.

He allowed himself one last look at Myr, then Ellie. He was still unsure about seeking a wishing tree, but he knew he had to do all he could for his family—he opened the front door of the house and slowly made his way outside into the cold morning. It wasn't like this was going to work anyway.

Handel reached into his hood pocket and pulled out the pale runestone. "What should I do with this?" he asked himself, impatiently. Eyes closed and runestone tight in hand, he commanded in a solemn voice, "Take me to the wishing tree." He opened his eyes and looked at the stone. It sat in his hand as pale and lifeless as before.

Handel's only prior experience seeing the effects of a runestone had been when a traveling troupe of performers stopped in Rondhill and showcased a trick in which a swordsman threw enchanted knives at a woman tied to a target. The knives burst into flame as they were thrown, each barely missing the woman. Perhaps this runestone was broken, he thought—or perhaps it was him. *Serves me right for getting swept up by that enchantress.* He briefly considered flinging the runestone away—seeing how far it could fly. But then he thought about the pleasantness of the runestone's smooth surface—the pleasure of running his thumb over it. He decided to hold onto it—if only for that purpose—and dropped it back into his cloak pocket.

What a waste of a morning, he sighed. And to start a workday already disappointed—Handel knew it was going to be a long day. He lowered his head, resigned, and marched through town on his way to work, his hand in his pocket fingering the runestone. He suddenly recalled there would be no wine given to them at lunch today, or any other day this week, and his feelings of dissatisfaction amplified. The need for drink grew as he passed *The Rat's Nest.* Alanda, the barmaid, was sweeping the entryway, preparing the tavern for the day. The place wouldn't open until Handel's workday had already begun, but that didn't stop him from pausing to stare wistfully at the tavern. Alanda noticed him and waved with a dimpled smile, her eyes dropping suddenly to his pocket.

"What do you have there?" she asked.

Handel wasn't sure what the woman was referring to until he looked down at his cloak pocket where a ghostly white glow was emanating through the fabric. He pulled out the runestone. No longer pale and dormant, a white light pulsed within the stone, consolidating into one side as if it were pointing him towards... *The Rat's Nest?*

Alanda had moved closer to him, her eyebrows raised in wonder. "That's not the sort of trinket I expected someone like you to carry," she said.

Handel's eyes remained fixed on the light within the stone. "It's supposed to guide me where I want to go," he murmured.

"Well, I'm flattered, but we won't open until later in the day," Alanda joked.

Handel flushed deeply and nodded at the young woman curtly, his eyes still concentrated on the stone. He found a quiet narrow alleyway behind the tavern and focused his mind. *The wishing tree. I need you to take me to the wishing tree.* The glow within the stone slowly moved from the tavern towards the woods outside of Pevine. Had this truly worked? Still skeptical, Handel made his way through the Pevine town square, where merchants were already setting up their wares for the morning market, and into the forest.

As he walked, the light would occasionally shift in a particular direction, at one point disappearing and changing direction entirely, pointing him back towards home when his mind strayed to thoughts of Ellie—he hadn't realized how responsive the stone was to his thoughts. He concentrated again, focusing on the wishing tree. The light in the stone adjusted itself once more.

As the sun rose into the clear sky, it did nothing to stifle the cold—this Winter was truly a brutal one. Handel found himself hungry and thirsty, but he kept his mind focused on the tree, just the tree and nothing else.

He walked through the woods for hours. He had never been this deep into the forest—the worksite being the farthest he had gone. Most townsfolk crossed the woods using what was known as the *Yellow Road*, named after the yellow sediment that formed it, and even then, only by cart. The road traveled north through the forest, then up the coast until it reached Perimat—the northernmost city of the Kingdom—that was a week's journey at least, even by horse. Handel had always dreamed of visiting all the major cities of the Kingdom, from Vizen to Mysa's Valley to the east and Amacore to the north. Why had his dream of travel died? *Because I lost my inn.* But an inn would have tied him down, not allowing him to leave. *Then because of Myr.* But Myr had always shared his love of travel. *Then because I must provide for my sick daughter.* But Ellie hadn't been sick as a babe; why hadn't he traveled then? *Then because...*

No matter, he had to remain focused. More hours passed following the runestone, and Handel began to question if the light was pointing him towards anything at all. He was no longer paying attention to his surroundings, his concentration narrowed to the pale glow of the stone. The woods grew thicker, impenetrable even, in some spots. How could woodsfolk live here? He was no tracker, but those large pawprints in the soft soil seemed like wolf prints to him. Ignoring them, he thought again of the tree—the last thing he needed was the light to guide him to the nearest *greatwolf.* A nearby bush was filled with red berries of the like Handel had never seen. His stomach grumbled sourly, but he knew not to pick berries he didn't recognize.

A strange hum filled the air—it was so quiet he wasn't certain if he was simply imagining it. The stone was almost filled with white light now, no longer pale but solidly bright. Handel stopped, his heart beating in his chest. He could feel a presence nearby silently watching him, just out of sight, breathing coldly on his neck. He felt his hands begin to shake and a knot twisting in his chest like snakes trying to escape from his lungs. He had arrived.

The clearing was wide and perfectly circular. The trees at the edge of the circle bent over as if gently bowing to the one in the middle. The tree at the center was old, perhaps as old as the forest itself. Its thin roots, like veins, were outstretched to the rest of the forest like ripples on a lake. Its branches were long and gnarled, as broad as the trunks of the other trees, and seemed to claw at the sky. A hollow in the middle of the tree stared at him like an empty eye socket. Handel felt his mouth dry up and his knees weaken.

The hum that filled the air was definitely real and, Handel was now certain, it was coming directly from the tree. He had heard woodsfolk speak of '*life energy*' before, but he had never had any context for what that might feel like.

He placed the almost blinding runestone in his cloak pocket and took a few uncertain steps towards the tree. The hum invited him to speak, but the words never found his mouth. He thought of Ellie, of her illness, searching for the strength to gather himself. When he finally found it, he said, "My daughter, Ellie." His voice was a barely audible whisper, but he could feel the tree listening—*a tree listening*. He couldn't make sense of it. But, somehow, he knew it to be true. "She's sick—dying. She means the world to me." He waited, part of him expecting the tree to say something back. When only the continuous *hum* came as an answer, he cleared his voice and continued, "Please... please save her."

The wind died, as did the sound of birds, and the rustling of leaves. The *hum* remained, drawing him to reach into the hole in the trunk. Handel knew exactly what that meant. *"...and I pulled out a knife,"* Myr had said. He walked towards the tree, slowly, until he was at arm's length from it. His whole body shook, the *hum* now seeming to fill his entire being. He hesitated for a moment. But then he felt the *hum*'s commanding energy—there was no turning back now. He reached a shaky hand into the dark eye of the tree and waited. The *hum* quieted, leaving his body. And then he felt it: something in his hand where moments ago there was nothing. He slowly pulled out his hand, expecting the worst.

He couldn't believe what he was seeing: five thick golden coins filled his hand. These weren't gold pieces but golden marks—the coins used by royals and nobles—more gold than he had seen after an entire year's hard work. With them, he could save his daughter *and* give his family the life they deserved.

Handel laughed loudly, hysterically even, as tears fell freely down his cheeks. He looked up at the tree, into its dark eye. The *hum* had quieted while the birds and the wind reprised their natural song. He wanted to say 'thank you' but the words died in his throat before they could make it out. He put the coins in his cloak pocket and, runestone in hand, thought of home, of Myr and Ellie smiling and laughing together. As he walked out of the clearing, he turned one last time. Defying all reason, he could no longer discern where the clearing had been. All the trees appeared the same. It was better that he did not return there. His eyes on the runestone, he pressed on through the forest.

Several hours went by before he saw another person, and it wasn't who he was expecting to see. Loggers cut down trees and transported them to woodworkers where they were shaped and sanded. Somehow, he had wandered into the worksite, at the end of the shift. He realized he had been thinking about work for the past hour or so, worried about having missed the day. Surely Brade would understand when he explained. Towards the center of the circle, near the *bore*, Brade sat on a stool closely examining a bucket full of black earth.

"Brade," Handel called out. The man didn't turn to look at him. "I know I'm late—"

"Late?" Brade's voice was calm, dangerously so. He continued, not looking away from his work, "Late is five, even ten minutes. That's late. The workday is almost done, and you were nowhere to be seen. Didn't I tell you to return today with a cool head?"

"Brade, I—"

"And I don't even care that you're a drunk," Brade interrupted, finally looking at him with an unreadable expression. "Half my men are drunks. It's useless men that I have no time for."

"Brade, I have a sick daughter—"

"I know all about your daughter, but if I am lenient towards you, as I have already been many times before, the other men will expect the same. No, don't embarrass yourself. My decision is final. You no longer have a place here." With that, Brade returned to his work, as if nothing had happened.

Handel's eyes drifted across the worksite. Several men shot him inquisitive glances; some shot mocking ones. He caught Tir looking at him, a shit-eating grin on his scarred face—the bruise on his jaw from the punch he received the day before was dark as a plum.

Handel took a step towards the foreman, lowering his voice to a whisper. "Brade. You have to help me."

"Go. Before I make you regret it."

"Please—"

Brade stood, locking eyes with Handel. "I'm only telling you to leave and not having you carried out by force because of our wives' friendship. Don't make me change my mind." Embarrassment reddened Handel's ears. He turned and walked out of the camp into the woods. The last sound he could make out was Brade barking at the workers to return to their duties.

It was dark when he arrived in Pevine, and cold—the sort that could bring a man to his knees. Handel's body ached, and hunger threatened to burn a hole through his stomach. A creeping headache at the back of his eyes reminded him it had been a whole day since he had had a drink. The healer's cabin was closed, and the chemist would also not open until morning.

From *The Rat's Nest*, he heard voices of merriment and drunken singing. Beads of sweat lined his forehead—strange since it was so cold. Perhaps he could warm himself in there. Just one mug of wine. He deserved it after all—he had walked more that day than he had all season. Before he could think it through, Handel had already stepped inside.

The tavern was bright and warm, several workmen filling the benches, plates full of roast chicken and mugs full of wine and ale. Some of the men grinned at him, while others went as far as to laugh. Handel didn't give them a second thought; he was of one mind right now. He stood at the bar and raised his hand to get Alanda's attention.

"What will it be?" she asked.

Handel reached into his cloak pocket for some pieces but found that it was empty except for the five gold marks. He felt the grooves on the coin where the sparrow crest of the royal family had been stamped. He couldn't think of one now, but he was sure there must be a woodsfolk saying about the dangers of flashing wealth in front of others. Against his better judgment, he slowly produced the coin and set it on the bar, barely lifting his hand enough for Alanda to catch sight of it.

"It's all I have," Handel murmured.

Alanda considered the coin with wide eyes. "Let me see if we can make change," she said, slightly annoyed. "If not, I can offer you credit."

The young woman walked through a door behind the bar. At the far end of the bar, two men were eyeing him. It wouldn't have bothered him—everyone in town spoke about him behind his back—except that he had never seen these two men before. They must have come for the afternoon market and stayed over for a drink or two. Slowly he slid the mark off the counter and returned it to his pocket. No one could have seen.

"I'm sorry, Handel," Alanda apologized—when had she returned? "We don't have enough for this tonight. Perhaps you can exchange it with a banker."

Those two men still had their eyes on him. He nodded a farewell to the young barmaid and hurried out of the tavern—he was sure there was still some wine left at home. Besides, he best make his way back and tell Myr and Ellie the good news. As he paced down the square, taking a turn through an alleyway, he heard footsteps behind him—one set it seemed. They mirrored his steps exactly, pacing when he paced, stopping when he stopped, turning when he turned. As they inched closer, he hastened his step, not daring to turn around. He was within ten minutes of home when suddenly he realized the steps had stopped. Only then did he turn—to find no one there. Had he imagined it? He really did need a drink.

Handel sighed in relief and continued forward. A man emerged from an alleyway in front of him, carelessly fingering the point of a long knife.

"Good evening," he said in a rough eastern accent. Handel balled his hands into fists, ready for a scuffle. "I would think of your next move very carefully," the man said coolly. Handel took a few steps back, then stopped when he felt something sharp prick his back lightly. Behind him stood the other man; he must have been hiding as the other one drove Handel into their trap. The lanterns were off, but he didn't have to see the men's faces to know they were the same ones from the pub.

"Give us your coin and you'll leave unscathed," the man behind him said. His breath smelled like rot.

Handel breathed deeply. He slowly reached into his pocket, pulled out a single gold coin, and handed it to the man behind him.

"Now, if we take a look in that pocket of yours, we won't find any more, right?" Handel felt sweat trickle down the side of his face. "Perhaps we'll give you a poke and find out."

"Please," Handel pleaded, trying to keep his voice level. "My daughter is sick. This is to buy her medicine."

"You take us for fools?" the man spat. "We saw you try to buy drink with that coin at the pub. Sick daughter, my arse."

Suddenly, pain bloomed at the back of his thigh where he was kicked, sending him falling to his knees. The man in front of him struck him across the brow with the butt of his knife. The men rummaged through his pockets while he lay in the mud, emptying them of the gold marks. One of the two men held onto the pale runestone, considering, but dropped it onto the ground when the other man called after him.

When Handel lifted his head, the men had vanished in the night, and with them, his daughter's life.

IX.

The Tree's Gift

The walk home was somber and slow. Handel was only dully aware of the wound at his back caused by the knife. No doubt he was bleeding under his shirt. The cold burned, but his mind was lost in a hazy pool. He had held his daughter's salvation in his hands and—just like that—let it go. He should have fought, even if it meant bleeding out in the mud. *Gods!* Why hadn't he fought? Dreams of leaving Pevine for the city with his wife and child evaporated in the frigid air like each puff of his hot breath. And for what? For one last lousy drink of wine. Handel imagined himself drowning in the stuff, suffocating, and dying. If he could give what was left of his miserable existence to Ellie, he would. She would make more of it than he could.

He stood in front of his house—he didn't remember reaching it nor how long he had been standing there. He didn't reach for the door handle—it might as well have been the mouth of a *spearhead* serpent. He jumped backward, startled as the door opened in front of him. Myr seemed equally as surprised to see him there.

"I thought I heard something," she said, with a gasp. All he could do was nod and walk inside. The warmth of the fireplace felt muted and miles away—the chill he felt could not be touched by it. Mechanically, he removed his boots and set them aside. He removed his frost-covered hood and set it in front of the fireplace to thaw. He could feel Myr's eyes piercing a hole in the back of his head, but he couldn't bring himself to face her. "I had a little talk with Yolta today. She apologized profusely for what Brade did. Obviously, I had no idea what she was referring to, so I asked." She let the words float in the air as if allowing him an opportunity to tell her what had happened. Handel remained quiet, holding the wet hood in front of the bright flames.

Myr continued, "As it turns out, you were kicked off the worksite yesterday for starting a fight, and you were a no-show today. She said Brade fired you." The haze grew thicker around his head, suffocating him. Myr took a few steps towards him, arms crossed—he didn't look at her face, but he could sense her anger. "And seeing as how you're coming home late today, no doubt, piss-drunk, with a blood-stained shirt—what do you have to say for yourself?"

Handel set the now dry hood over the back of a nearby chair. He finally faced Myr. To his horror, there wasn't a trace of anger on her face, only sadness, and exhaustion. He tried to speak but it sounded more like a sigh. "I—"

"Papa!" The two parents turned towards the small voice. Ellie stood outside her room, holding herself on the wall. Instead of waiting for her to run to him, Handel hurried towards her and hoisted her into his arms. "Come tell me a story, Papa," she said weakly.

"Ellie, your father and I are speaking," Myr said, struggling to keep her voice firm. "And what did I tell you about leaving your bed by yourself?"

"I wanted to see Papa," the girl said.

"Ellie—"

"I went to the wishing tree," Handel said.

It was as if time itself had stopped—even the sound of the crackling fireplace felt muffled. Ellie's arms wrapped themselves tightly around his neck. He hugged her back, but his eyes remained focused on Myr. Her expression was blank and unreadable. He wanted her to do something, to say something, but she just stood there, staring at him as her eyes welled up with tears. "You did what?" she finally asked, stunned.

"That's why I missed work." Handel's voice trembled. *What are you saying, you fool?* "I did it."

"Oh, Papa," Ellie giggled. "I'm going to feel good again?"

Handel brushed her hair. "Yes, Ellie. You'll be better very soon."

Myr's face seemed frozen in an incredulous stare, but the tears that fell from her eyes betrayed her. She took a few unsure steps towards her husband and child, before rushing forward to embrace them heavily. She cried and cried, and so did he—albeit for a different reason. She thanked him and kissed him all over his face, as did Ellie. For the first time in so long, he felt as if he had truly done something for his family. It was a lie. *You are lower than the lowest scum. A piece of shit to be scraped off a boot. How can you do this to them? How can you even live with yourself?*

When they put Ellie to bed, she fell asleep almost instantly. The excitement wore her out. Myr cleaned the wound at Handel's back with attentive and loving fingers. She never asked where he got it—why did that bother him? Once the wound was tended to, Myr dragged her mat next to Handel's. For a while, she stared at him, twirling his beard hairs with her slender finger. He couldn't remember the last time he had felt her body so close, so warm and soft, the sweet smell of sweat and Winter emanating from her—it was almost overwhelming. Before he knew it, she had fallen asleep with her head on his chest, her back rising and falling with each slow breath. This was a reminder of what he had been denying himself by being a drunken waste. Yet, he couldn't bring himself to enjoy it.

He had lied to his family. Ellie was going to die, and it was all because of him. He turned his head away from Myr—he couldn't bear to look at her, so beautiful and perfect, like the day they first met. His eyes fell on his hood, hanging over the chair, its inner pocket bulging where the runestone was stored.

No, that's crazy, he thought, suppressing the idea that crept at the back of his head. One could only receive a gift from the wishing tree once. That was the rule that woodsfolk lived by when wishing trees were found more easily through the forest—or so the woodsfolk stories claimed. Whether it was a real rule or simply superstition, Handel had never cared. But now, he wasn't hoping to find out. He closed his eyes, praying to the gods that sleep might come, but somehow his gaze kept returning to the pocket.

He slowly moved Myr's head aside, placing it gently on the mat, and stood up. He tip-toed over to the hood and pulled out the runestone. As he held it, a light formed within, consolidating slowly to a single point. He didn't have to wonder where it might be pointing—he knew it was the tree.

He felt sick to his stomach, his head spinning. Was he really going to go through with this? Before he could think it over, he had donned his shirt and trousers, Winter hood, and boots.

"Where are you going?" Myr asked groggily.

Handel froze. He wanted nothing more than to remove his clothes and return to bed with the mother of his child and love of his life. How had he forgotten his feelings towards her for so long? "I just need some fresh air," he said.

Myr stretched with a gentle grunt and pulled the covers over herself. "Please, come back soon."

"I will," he lied, opening the door, the cold hitting his face like a slap.

"I love you," she said. How long had it been since he heard those words?

"I love you too." The words felt familiar, like a childhood catechism he had once known by heart. He stepped into the cold and gently closed the door. There was no turning back now; his mind was made, or was it simply desperation? He pulled the runestone from his pocket and held it, waiting for the light to point him forward. To his surprise, the light pointed behind him, back to his home, to his wife and daughter. How had he allowed himself to become so distanced from those he loved? Wine had erected a fence between them—one that grew taller with every drink. Tonight, Handel had crossed that barrier for the first time in years. Filling his lungs with freezing air, he concentrated on the tree. The light in the runestone moved, pointing towards the forest.

With nothing but the moon and stars above him and the light from the runestone to guide his way, the woods were very dark. But Handel didn't have time to consider the danger. A few miles in, he slipped on a smooth rock and about fell arse over head into the mud. Keeping his eyes on the runestone and the dark road ahead, he pressed on. Another mile in, the woods became even darker and much thicker. Handel contemplated the sky: pale clouds had swallowed the moon, blocking its light. The coldness and dampness in the air threatened ill weather—but that would have to be a worry for later.

It took much longer to reach the clearing the second time—perhaps because of the darkness. However, Handel had an uncanny impression that the clearing had been elsewhere, more westward. But there was no way the clearing could have moved. Handel's heavy breath came out in white puffs. Strangely, it had gotten colder as he neared the tree. The *hum* was still there, but much softer, dormant. Handel placed the bright runestone in his cloak and walked towards the tree. The fear he felt the first time was gone, replaced instead by a strange sense of foreboding. No one was allowed to ask the tree for a second wish. But he had to try.

"Hello," he said, immediately feeling stupid for having said it. "I know I was here before... And I know I'm not supposed to ask twice. Well, here I am..." The *hum* continued, quiet and dull as if the tree were listening. "It's my daughter, Ellie... I was careless—a fool. I threw away the one chance I had at seeing her healed. It's all my fault—all because of my selfishness," he clenched his fists. "But if I do nothing, she will surely die." Unbidden tears filled his eyes. Handel fell to his knees, slowly crawling closer to the tree. "Please, help me. No. Help her, in any way you see fit. Please. Please..."

Handel's pleading turned into quiet sobs. When he managed to compose himself somewhat, he noticed that the wind had subsided, along with the night sounds that had filled the forest moments before. The *hum* grew louder, beckoning him to move closer. *Could it be?* Could the tree be willing to grant him a second wish?

Slowly, he stood up, his stomach twisting in anticipation. His hand moved closer to the dark eye of the tree. Closer. Closer. Until, at last, it was in. He shut his eyes, waiting for the worst. But nothing came.

Suddenly, the *hum* quieted. The wind began to blow again, and the night sounds returned. Handel removed his hand from the hole. Empty. No. Handel looked closely. There was something on his hand: a small black dot, like a dark pimple, protruding from the center of his palm. He tried rubbing it off with his thumb, but it felt as if it were part of him. He looked up at the tree, but its *voice* remained silent—that was reason enough to leave this place. The quest had been a failure. Snow began to fall softly.

Within minutes, the forest was covered in powdery white. Handel reached for the runestone to guide his way home. As he looked at it, he noticed his hand again. A strange green substance was sprouting from the small black dot on his palm. It was fuzzy and soft, very much like moss. His eyes widened as he watched it grow, until it covered his entire hand, then his arm, climbing up to his shoulder. In a panic, he dropped the runestone to the ground and ran as fast as he could through the dark woods. Part of him knew where he was headed. The rest was filled with terror. The moss reached to his neck, his face, and down his legs now. His arm was covered in rough bark that made his motions stiff. Something caught on his boot and he fell face-first into the mud and snow. He looked at his foot, fearing it broken, only to see what appeared to be roots bursting through his boots and reaching into the ground. He tried to stand, but the roots that emerged from under his fingernails were intent on embedding themselves into the dirt.

With the little breath he had left, Handel cried out, "I don't care about me, but please have mercy on my daughter. I am nothing, but she needs to live. She has to live!"

A strange calm came over him. He heard it then, the *hum*, gentle and lulling. It was coming from all around him. The trees were singing sleepily, as was the snow and the air itself. High-pitched *shrieks*, both near and far, seemed to harmonize with the song. It was the most beautiful sound Handel had ever heard. He felt himself slither out of the dirt, his roots retreating. Then, on his arm, he saw a berry grow, red as blood. Then another berry, and another, until he was covered. Had anyone walked by, they no doubt would have confused him with a berry bush. He plucked a berry between his bark-covered fingers and squeezed it. He couldn't be certain how, but he knew what he must do.

❦ ❦ ❦ ❦

Ellie woke shivering. She rubbed the sleep from her eyes as she looked around her room. It was dark, the candle having burnt out long before. She always preferred to fall asleep with it lit—the dark frightened her. Papa had told her once that there was no reason to fear the dark, as everything was just the same as it was during the day. She had a hard time believing that—the planks of wood that formed her ceiling were normal during the day, but in the shadowy night they took on many different forms: an eyeless man, a crow eating a baby, and the worst one of all, a grinning *greatwolf*. The light of a candle made all those shapes vanish. She normally would have called for Momma to light the candle again, but Ellie didn't want to wake her—she had been working so hard since Papa had been returning home late every day. She deserved some rest.

Ellie turned to the window. The curtains blew in the cold wind. An eerie glow filled the night from the freshly fallen snow. She liked the way snow looked, but she didn't very much like the feel of it, how it made everything wet and cold. How did that window come to be open? She recalled her mother closing it in the evening. She tried to move from the bed with no success. Something was holding her down, but in the darkness, she couldn't see what. She blindly felt her way towards the end of the bed until she came upon something rough, like a branch covered in something soft and damp. As her eyes adjusted to the darkness, she could make out the shape of something large and dark standing at the foot of her bed. She gasped, and the shape moved closer.

"It's all right, Ellie," the shape said. The voice sounded somewhat familiar. "It's Papa." The shape looked nothing like Papa, but it did sound like him, only rougher—perhaps he had been out drinking again. Momma didn't like it when Papa drank.

"I can't see you. Papa, can you light the candle?" Ellie asked.

The shape barely moved. "No, my dear," he said. Something was wrong; she could sense it. "Here, Ellie. The wishing tree gave me this medicine to give you. The tree said it will heal you, make you stronger." The shape held something between its fingers—if that's what they could be called.

"Oh, Papa! I'm so happy," said Ellie excitedly. The shadow dropped something into her outstretched hands. The small object was round and soft.

"Eat it," he said. His voice was becoming deeper and stranger. *Perhaps Papa has a cold.* Ellie put the small sphere in her mouth and bit down on it: it popped against her tongue like a berry, but the flavor was like no berry she had ever tried before. It tasted like sucking on a fresh wound to stop the bleeding. Suddenly, a strange warmth bloomed in her limbs, and her head spun. Before she knew it, she fell back onto her pillow, her eyes closed heavily. She entered a sleep plagued with strange dreams of a singing forest. On the other side of this forest was a lake of blood. Papa was in the lake, thrashing as he drowned. She reached out for him, *"Papa, take my hand!"* But he only smiled and allowed the blood to swallow him.

Ellie shot up, covered in sweat. She had had fevers before, but none that felt so... refreshing? More than that: she felt well, strong. The feeling of it made her realize how weak she had been for so long. Then it came to her—a memory that felt as if it were part of her dream: Papa had come to her and said the tree would heal her. She got out of bed quickly and with incredible ease. The strength she felt now made her giddy with joy. She glanced out of the window: it was still early morning, but it must have snowed all night seeing as the entire neighborhood appeared covered in a thick white blanket. She bolted out of her room and to where Myr still lay asleep.

"Momma! Momma!" she cried out.

Myr sprung up as Ellie jumped up and down on Handel's empty mat. "Ellie? Why are you out of bed?"

"Because I'm not sick anymore!" she yelled—no, proclaimed. "The wishing tree healed me thanks to Papa!"

Myr seemed incredulous. She grabbed Ellie to stop her from jumping, checking the girl's forehead and ear for fever. She checked and double-checked several times, her face morphing gradually from anger to astonishment. Then the tears came. "True One be blessed, he really did it." Myr hugged Ellie tight and kissed her all over. The girl begged her to stop between giggles. Then, suddenly, Myr stopped to look around the house. "Handel? she called.

When there was no reply, Ellie said, "I don't think Papa is here."

Myr looked troubled. She stood from her mat and searched the living area, for Handel's hood and boots. Both were missing. Then she opened the front door and called out, "Handel! Handel?" No response. Ellie ran out of the house quickly and frolicked in the snow, barefoot. "Ellie! Come back! What are you doing running out into the cold in your nightgown with no shoes?" she tutted.

"Catch me, Momma!" Ellie ran through the snow, entirely unbothered by the cold and too excited by being able to do so to stop. Myr chased her down—angrily at first, but eventually, Ellie could hear her mother's giggles between her calls of admonishment.

Ellie didn't care—she had spent too many years of her childhood in that bedroom, in that bed, coughing and wheezing. She had never been able to run or be outside for so long; she didn't want it to end.

As Ellie turned the corner behind the house, she stopped. Myr caught up to her and swaddled the child in her warm arms. "What has gotten into you?" Myr said, still playfully—she was much too happy to be angry.

Ellie pointed ahead. "Was that always there?"

Myr stared at the tree that stood in the small space between their home and their neighbors' and shook her head in confusion. Ellie shrugged out of her mother's grasp and ran to the tree. "Ellie, seriously," Myr called, "you have to put something on if you're going to be outside."

Ellie stood in front of the tree, watching it closely. Something about it felt strange to her. She could feel a faint sadness emanating from it, like a *hum*. Its branches were dripping with red berries; its trunk was gnarled into many strange shapes—one of them like an oddly familiar face.

Myr took Ellie by the arm and turned her. "Come on," she said. "Let's go inside and get some proper Winter clothes on you. Then we can go out and play until your father returns home."

Ellie nodded and followed her mother back inside.

SPRING:
A Foreman

X.

Black Air

Twins were seen as a blessing in Albadone. When Eicko and Brade were born it seemed as if the entire woodsfolk community gathered to celebrate, with three solid days of drinking, dancing, merriment, and a myriad of games. Even travelers and townsfolk that found themselves in the woods during that time were swept up in the fun. Recounting those days, the boys' mother lamented she would have preferred a quiet celebration followed by some much-needed rest—but that was not how things were done in Albadone. The festivities ended with the traditional introduction of the twins to the woodsfolk: the boys were placed in a woven basket, which was passed from neighbor to neighbor as a sign of luck and goodwill. Chants were then lifted to the True One, and the exhausted mother was at last left to her recovery.

Eicko had come out first, and thus he was the eldest by woodsfolk tradition. Brade was second, gripping tightly onto his brother's foot. Their youth was spent much the same—Eicko leading, with his younger brother following reluctantly behind. Despite being twins, the two boys couldn't have been more different in appearance. Eicko had fiery red hair and a slender build, his face long and fair. Brade, on the other hand, was stocky and short, his hair smooth and black. No one that saw them would have ever taken them for brothers, much less twins.

It was a warm Spring day when Eicko found the chasm. Brade had misbehaved that morning, so their father had set him to work pulling weeds in the garden. In truth, it had been Eicko's idea to steal from Yeima's apple tree, but, as usual, it was Brade who had been clumsy enough to be caught. The two boys had an agreement: if one of them was caught, then he must bear the punishment alone. Unfortunately for Brade, he was caught far more often than Eicko, which, he often claimed, was horribly unfair. Eicko, on the other hand, quite liked their agreement.

Eicko had a knack for stealth and speed. His favorite use of these talents was for adventuring, which was what he set out into the woods for that afternoon, leaving his brother to his punishment. He reached the banks of the Chleo river—which functioned as a sort of border that their mother forbade them to cross. Deciding to test his luck again, he began wading across it. The shallow water was cool and crisp—a welcome respite from the afternoon heat. Once on the other bank, Eicko laughed to himself, proudly defiant of his mother's warning. Ahead of him was unexplored terrain. Although it looked much like the woods he left behind the novelty and nervous excitement of being where he wasn't supposed to be propelled Eicko forward. He would have to remember where the Chleo ran—he wasn't about to lose his way home. He moved through the woods, which grew thicker and more lush as he traveled deeper into them.

He passed a small homestead that he promptly avoided in case it was inhabited by somebody his parents knew—being caught disobeying his mother was the last thing he wanted. Not much else in the scenery changed after that, and he soon grew bored and decided he would keep walking until the sun reached the tops of the trees ahead, then turn back. Perhaps he would even head home and tease Brade for a while—but only if he truly had nothing better to do.

Just as he was about to call it a day, he noticed that the grass under his feet had become thin and sparse. The roots of the trees around him now were gnarled and exposed, their tops spindly and barren of any foliage. Eicko dug into the ground with his hand: immediately he exposed a hard, rocky surface beneath the thin layer of dirt. His interest was piqued. Most of Albadone was covered in soft soil—he knew this especially after the past Summer when he and Brade had dug a huge hole and flooded it with well water in an attempt to create their own fishing hole. He had never seen their father so livid.

Still feeling the hard ground under his feet, he reached a spot where the grass had given up entirely. There, between the intertwined roots of two unfortunate looking trees was a small chasm—a crack in the earth. Eicko crouched to look in, but the darkness below was impenetrable. A strange sour smell wafted from its depths, like the breath of a drunk. Eicko slid one foot into the chasm, then another, and finally the rest of him followed. The hole seemed to lead deeper down, perhaps into a cavern. Excitement bubbled in Eicko's head—he couldn't wait to show Brade what he had found. He didn't like admitting it, but everything was more fun with his younger twin. He stopped himself from going any further, as it was much too dark. Instead, he climbed back out with ease and began running towards home.

It was late afternoon when he finally reached the cabin, and around the time of day when their mother was just beginning to wonder where he was. Brade was still in his work clothes busy weeding the garden, his face a mess of dirt and sweat. Eicko ran up to him. "Brade!" he called out between panting breaths. "I found a hole in the woods."

"That's nice," Brade replied, doing his best to ignore his brother.

"It's really narrow and dark, but we can both fit. I think it might lead into a cave." Brade ripped the weeds out of the ground with growing intensity. "Are you upset with me?" Eicko asked.

"Of course not," Brade said, venomously. "I'm so happy I get to work the garden all day while you run around looking for holes." His hand tore the weeds out now with a sort of relish. "I'm just ecstatic I get to be punished for something that was entirely your idea. Especially since I don't even like Yeima's rotten old apples."

"Come on, Brade. We both came up with that scheme."

"Oh, no you don't! Last I checked, I wasn't the one who shook *myself* awake this morning to tell *myself* about how much *I* desired an apple tart. This was all *your* plan. They're always *your* plans, and *I'm* always the one who gets caught." Brade pulled a weed out of the ground and tossed it at Eicko, sending soft soil flying everywhere. Eicko took a step back, the fistful of wet dirt and weeds landing at his feet.

"What do we always say? If you get caught it's your fault."

Brade sighed. "I know. It's only... it would be nice to not *always* be the one who gets caught."

Eicko couldn't blame him. He had to admit, most of their schemes were of his device—if not all. Eicko shook his head and knelt on the ground, next to his brother. "How much do you have left?"

Brade's face brightened. "Just this last row."

Eicko reached for a nearby weed and tugged until it popped out of the ground, his younger twin's eyes still on him, full of surprise. "Don't get any strange ideas," Eicko admonished. "Our rule still stands. Next time you're caught you're on your own." Brade agreed and returned to work. "And, since you owe me, you'll have to come with me to that cave tomorrow."

Brade nodded. "Whatever you say."

At dinner, their father showed displeasure that Eicko had helped his brother but was relieved that the work was finished at least. The man wasn't much for cooperation—he believed a man forged his own path and, thus, must face his destiny alone. Eicko thought that was a load of shit, but he would never say that to their father's face. He did not speak a word to his parents about the chasm—the less they knew about his schemes the better.

The next morning, Eicko awoke groggily—he had barely slept due to the prospect of a new adventure. The twins had explored the surrounding woods to the point where they knew them better than their mother's voice. Discovering a new place opened the door to so many enticing possibilities. Images of ancient dragon's gold and mysterious hidden cities flashed through his imagination. Whatever that chasm led to, it was going to be his. He washed his face in the cold well water his mother kept in a basin by the door and headed outside, followed closely by his younger twin. They moved towards the shed where their father kept his work supplies.

"What are we doing here?" Brade asked once they were inside. Daylight through the cracked front door cut the shed in half. Hoes, rakes, and other gardening supplies were scattered about the floor. Shelves lined the walls, filled with all sorts of tools and miscellaneous wares, from tacks to dried meats. Eicko rummaged about some shelves until he produced a small metal object. "What is that?" Brade asked.

"Father's firestarter," Eicko answered.

"True One! What do we need that for?" Eicko ignored his brother and hurried out of the shed into the nearby woods. Brade joined him a few moments later—the boy was so slow! "This is always how I get caught," Brade huffed, his face reddened by the run—or maybe just the anger. "I ask about your scheme and you run off without answering. Do you want me to be part of this, or not?"

Eicko grabbed his brother's shoulder to calm him down. "I'm sorry Brade. I'll try to be more considerate." His voice came out a bit more mocking than he intended.

"It's all right." But from the boy's tone, it clearly wasn't.

Eicko held the firestarter in front of Brade's face—a circle made of thin metal that fit comfortably in the palm of a hand with two sets of flint teeth. Eicko squeezed the firestarter and, with a metallic click, sparks jumped from where the teeth collided. "The cave is really dark. With this, we'll be able to light the way." That seemed to appease Brade's curiosity, at least until they reached the river.

"Mother said we shouldn't cross the Chleo," Brade protested as Eicko was already making his way across.

"And yet—" Eicko chuckled as he picked his way through the cold water. Brade remained rooted on the other bank, arms crossed. "What is it? Are you scared?" Eicko taunted.

"No..." Brade sighed. "I'm simply preparing myself for when I'm eventually caught and punished for this. For how many years do you think they'll starve me?"

Eicko doubled over with laughter. "They won't starve you, silly! Come on!"

Brade sighed and waded to the other bank, complaining the entire time. Once across, Eicko mussed his brother's hair—Brade hated when he did that—and continued leading the way through the woods. This time he was careful to avoid the nearby homestead entirely. It was best if Brade didn't know there was even the remotest possibility of being caught by a neighbor. After a long stroll, they reached the area where the grass grew sporadically and the trees seemed desperate to prop themselves out of the earth. Eicko searched the area for a few moments, initially unsure of where the chasm had been. Something brushed his nose—that peculiar sour smell. He closed his eyes and followed it until he stood where the two trees' roots tangled together. "Here it is!" he exclaimed.

Upon seeing the chasm, Brade tilted his head skeptically. "It's so... small."

"I told you it was," Eicko said. "But it's wide enough for us to go inside, I already made sure."

Brade got on his knees and looked into the dark slit. His nose wrinkled, and he sneezed into his sleeve. "What is that horrible smell?"

"Ogre farts," Eicko joked.

Brade did his best not to laugh at that, but even he couldn't stop himself from cracking a smile. "All right, we've seen it. Now can we go back?"

"Absolutely out of the question!" Eicko exclaimed. "We are going in."

"Are not!" Brade protested, standing. "You can go in there if you'd like, but I'm staying out here."

Eicko sighed. "Fine. I'll go in and you'll be lookout in case somebody comes around."

"Who would come around?" Brade asked, looking alertly at their surroundings.

Eicko rolled his eyes. "No one! I'm trying to give you something to do while I discover all this treasure." Eicko ripped a branch from a nearby tree and handed it to Brade.

"What's this for?" Brade asked.

Eicko produced the firestarter from his pocket and handed it over as well. "When I'm inside, light this like a torch and hand it to me. I can't bring it in with me through the hole while it's lit."

"I don't think this is how torches work," Brade complained—he just had to complain about everything.

Eicko ignored his brother's comment—although, on second thought, he probably did have a point—and headed into the chasm. He put one foot in, then the other, and then slid through until his entire body was inside. As he slid deeper into the hole, the opening widened until it felt almost comfortable to lie in. The smell was stronger inside, but Eicko had already grown accustomed to it. It was almost pleasant even. Almost.

"Pass me the torch!" Outside he could hear Brade fiddling with the firestarter, struggling to produce a spark.

Perhaps I should have done that part before descending, he thought. "Do you need help?" asked Eicko, a bit of mockery spicing his voice.

"I can do this," Brade shot back, irritated. Eicko snickered as the clicking sound of the firestarter continued. Eventually, the clicking stopped and Brade exclaimed, "I got it lit!"

Eicko lifted his arm until his hand poked out of the ground like another sad tree. "Hand the torch here," he said. He curled his fingers around the wood when he felt it touch his hand and pulled the torch into the chasm. Hot white light surrounded him, and the air left his lungs in an instant as he drowned in it.

※ ※ ※ ※

The sounds of the worksite felt muffled and distant. Brade sat on the riverbank, tinkering with a small contraption he had built—the prototype for a new sort of lantern. He didn't like to tell people that he had first seen this device in a dream, but that was the truth. If it worked the way it was supposed to, it would harness the power of the *black air*, turning it into light—Brade wasn't sure which one of the workers had started calling it that, but the name had caught on. One day, perhaps, all the candle lanterns in Pevine would be replaced with these.

His prototype was almost finished—a glass chimney containing a wool mesh that incandesced when the *black air* was lit—but he still hadn't worked out how to collect the foul-smelling *air*. The wooden barrels he had his workers build were too porous, allowing the *air* to escape freely moments after it was captured. His latest design had been of a steel barrel with a lid that compressed the *air*, keeping it safely inside. The smiths had worked out the steel barrels within a week but placing those lids on without any *air* escaping had been a particular struggle.

Brade dreamed often of *black air* bursting into flame, lighting the world. Other times, he dreamed of his brother Eicko's face materializing within the stuff and then being swallowed by fire as it had all those years past. It wasn't something he wished to remember, but he couldn't help it—the image of his brother's face peeking out of those white flames came to him, as it always did, unbidden, instantly returning him to that terrible day. Fire had poured out of the chasm for several days after the accident, eventually being put out by heavy rain—nothing had remained of his twin brother.

As the years passed, Brade often found himself returning to the chasm. He could feel his brother's presence there. He knew it was strange, but the place brought him a sense of comfort. Brade reached in his pocket—he did so instinctively when thoughts of his brother crept in. He felt the thin metal firestarter that he had carried ever since that day—a reminder. And a promise.

Now the *bore* stood where the chasm once was. The huge wooden structure was, in part, a monument to his twin's death and, in part, a monument to progress. It had taken Brade years, but, at last, his dreams were close to becoming reality. He would harness the destructive power of the *black air* into something useful. What he wanted most was to dig into the earth and find the *air's* origin. Perhaps then his brother's death would find purpose.

"You're going to kill us all," a young woman's voice said softly behind him.

Brade didn't have to turn to know who it was. "Mother Adriel." He greeted her wryly. "To what do I owe the pleasure?"

"You should know what I want by now," she replied in a level tone.

"And *you* should know by now that I am not going to destroy the *bore* simply because you have a bad feeling," Brade said, careful to match the enchantress's casual tone. The young enchantress had been harassing him for weeks now. She really made him miss Mother Olla, the old enchantress that had been the young woman's teacher—at least the old woman had never so much as spoken a word to him.

Mother Adriel sat, legs crossed, on a nearby boulder, facing Brade. She folded her hands in front of her, a picture of serenity—Brade knew it was all for show. "Have you ever heard of the Guardians of Albadone?"

Brade rolled his eyes. "I am a woodsman, aren't I?"

The enchantress chuckled softly as if to ask, 'are you?' The expression on her face quickly chilled. "The True One made the *mers* to guard the rivers and lakes, the *griffons* to guard the heavens, the *dragons* to guard the mountains, and the *melk* to guard the forest," she recited solemnly as if quoting something. "But when folk settled into Albadone, they drove the Guardians away with violence, thus sealing the fate of the forest in blood."

Brade set aside his lantern, finally looking directly at the woman. Her hood was pulled back, revealing her wild brown hair—had it always been so messy? "Thank you for refreshing me on my own people's history," Brade said. "I'll make sure to recount it to my sons the next time they ask me for a bedtime story."

The woman smiled defiantly. "The Guardians sense a danger in Albadone, one that may kill us all if left unstopped."

"Get to your point, enchantress."

"Beneath Albadone lies its lifeblood, and the *melk* have returned to defend it. The lifeblood calls out to them, and if you don't cease your digging soon, they will find you and they will kill you and every other man, woman, and child that inhabits these woods."

It took a few moments for Brade to realize he had balled his hands into white-knuckled fists. "Please leave me be," he pleaded to the young woman, attempting to relax his hands and shoulders.

Mother Adriel smoothed her skirt, her head shaking. "*Ulfer's* arse, you're a stubborn fool." She hopped off the boulder. "I've done my part in warning you. Now it's up to you to do the right thing." And with that, the young enchantress disappeared into the thick woods.

Brade spat. It took him a few moments to collect himself—the enchantress irked him to no end. At first, she appeared at the worksite to discourage the workers from their duties—that was until Brade hired guardsmen to patrol the perimeter of the worksite with specific instruction to keep her out. Then, the woman had started approaching him while he took his lunch break in the woods. Soon, he thought, she may well appear in his dreams to condemn him. Woodsfolk custom dictated that enchantresses were to be held in high regard, but Brade had had enough of these false pleasantries. The next time he saw the woman near him, he wouldn't be so polite. The world he was creating had no use for that sort of nonsense.

A distant shout from the worksite called him back to the present. His first thought was, *what has that enchantress done now?* Thankfully, the shouts seemed to be happy ones, excited even. He picked up the lantern and quickly made his way to the worksite.

XI.

Black Water

The sour smell streamed out from below the *bore* in waves. Many of the workers had told Brade that, after the first few months working there, they had grown used to the odor and no longer noticed it. That never happened to him—he could smell the *black air* from a distance, even after spending all day in it so that the smell blanketed him like an aura. This had been helpful several years ago when Brade's 'purse in Vizen'— Brade's nickname for the unknown wealthy benefactor who funded his venture—had him set out across Albadone in search of more chasms and sources of *black* air. He had found several scattered throughout the woods but ultimately decided to have the *bore* constructed at the site of Eicko's disappearance.

The smell that came from the well this morning was thicker, more concentrated. The workers were gathered around the *bore*, some cheering, others muttering confusedly. There was a general sense of excitement that pervaded the site, and it showed on each worker's face. Brade knew each of those faces very well. He was adamant that it was vital for a foreman to handpick his workers. He always took time to meet and get to know each of them, even going so far as to invent simple rhymes to help him remember their names.

Brade didn't have to push his way through the crowd to get to the well—as soon as the workers saw him, they parted to allow him passage. All eyes turned to him, as Brade reached the *bore*. Ered—*whose hair is fire-red*—the young woodsfolk, sat on the stone mouth of the well, his face and arms coated in black sludge. The youngster breathed heavily with some sort of strain, but a toothy white grin sat wide on his face. In front of him was a bucket full of shiny black liquid, the same type that covered the lad.

"Master Brade," Ered greeted giddily, still smiling. He nodded towards the bucket. Brade dipped his finger in the thick black liquid. It felt neither warm nor cool, somewhere in between. It was slimy, but not sticky. Brade filled his nostrils with its sour smell, and a wool-like warmth wafted through his head. He felt lightheaded and dizzy, but only for a moment. Then, suddenly, a thought.

"Is the pipe—" Brade didn't even need to finish for Ered's smile to grow wider. Brade paced towards the other side of the well, the workers parting before him as a court would for a king. He reached for the rope ladder mounted on the side of the stone well, and climbed down deep into the earth, under the *bore*. Steel pipes ran down the side of the well into the depths below.

As Brade descended, an eerie blue and purple glow illuminated his path downward. It had been weeks since the last time Brade had gone into the shaft, and he was almost startled by the progress his workers had made. Yona—*with the unpleasant aroma*—the head miner, kept him updated daily on their excavations, but to see it with his own eyes was astounding. The opening of the well stood over one hundred feet above him, daylight struggling to leak in. Several tunnels had been dug in different directions, each of their walls lined with steel pipes that converged at the center of the shaft into the *sifter*—a large steel container of Brade's invention that would be used to force the *black air* to the surface once he had figured out the storage issue. On the shaft walls were glass bottles full of *dreadhalls*—the glowing mushrooms that illuminated the space with their purple-blue luster; Brade had been very adamant that fire was not to be allowed anywhere near the *bore*.

Some miners stood about, seemingly unsure of what their orders were. Others wiped themselves clean with wet rags, their bodies dirtied by the black liquid. Yona stood next to the *sifter*. His wispy black and gray beard struggled to hide what was an unusually ugly face. What the barrel-chested man lacked in looks, however, he very much made up for in hard work and honesty.

"Brade, over here," Yona called out.

When Brade reached the *sifter*, he noticed the strange sound it was producing—like a muffled river or a distant mudslide. "What's going on with the *sifter*?"

"Take a look for yourself," Yona answered. The burly man lifted the lid off the top of the device with his thick hairy arms—how he did that was always a marvel to Brade; the thing must have weighed fourteen stone. In the device, Brade could see that the black liquid was slowly being pumped from the pipes into the machine.

"What is this? How did this come about?" Brade asked, feeling wary and unsure.

"The north-western tunnel system reached another shaft below," Yona explained. "When the pressured pipe burst through the shaft wall, that black stuff came pouring in. We had to close the valve or else we would have filled the entire shaft with it." Brade's eyes remained fixed on the liquid. "What do you think it is?" Yona asked.

Brade hadn't even considered the question: to him, it was quite obvious. "This is what we've been searching for. Just as steam turns to water when it collects, *black air* turns to—"

"*Black water,*" Yona interrupted.

"*Black water,*" Brade repeated, nodding. "It would seem we have solved our storage problem."

"So, what shall we do with it?"

Brade's hand began to tremble involuntarily—wariness had made way for a flood of excitement. "Let's bring it to the surface."

"Aye." Yona placed the lid back on the *sifter* and headed towards a group of miners.

As Brade made his way up the rope ladder, he could hear the booming of Yona's orders bouncing off the shaft walls. His arms felt tired and worn by the time he was out. One of the workers, Yase—*with a nose like a vase*—helped him out. The excitement Brade still felt was a welcome distraction from the pulsating strain in his limbs. Nearby he noticed Peter—*the pickled parsnip eater*—a smart, strong, and seasoned woodsman that had helped Brade design the *bore*. Brade pointed at him and called, "To the wheel! It's time!" The man smiled and dashed to a ladder in the interior of the *bore*'s wooden tower. He climbed to a platform where a large vertical wooden wheel was placed, connected to a system of ropes and pulleys that reached into the well. "On my word, turn it."

Brade directed his attention to the workers that were gathered around. "I need a barrel at the pump. No, bring two, just in case. And stand aside as it could get messy." Six men ran to where the barrels were stacked and rolled two of them towards the well pump that stood a few feet away from the *bore*. Brade's heart was beating heavily in his chest. This was his life's work—no, his and Eicko's. Soon, he would shine a light, brightening the path to a new Albadone.

"Now!" he yelled, and Peter began turning the wheel. At first, it seemed like it wouldn't budge, but after some force, it began to turn freely. The ropes wiggled, and the sound of pressure releasing like steam in a kettle ran up and down the *bore*. Brade faced the men at the pump. "Pump, now!" he ordered. Brinn—*with the mole on his chin*—pushed down on the pump and, without so much as a warning, the *black water* began to flow freely into the barrel. Workers rolled over a few more barrels, predicting some overflow.

Even after Brade ordered the wheel closed, the *water* continued to flow, filling three barrels fully and part of a fourth. The workers cheered as they watched—they couldn't have had any idea of what the accomplishment meant, but they could tell by looking at Brade that whatever had happened was good. Even the miners came out from beneath the well to watch, their dirty faces making their smiles appear even brighter. Once the *water* finally did stop flowing from the pump and the barrels were shut, Brade spent a moment taking in all that had happened. The workers' eyes were all on him, expectant. Brade stood atop a nearby pile of planks, facing them all. Silence descended upon the worksite in anticipation of the foreman's words.

"Workers," he began. "Today we have accomplished the impossible." He knew what he needed to express, but the words were eluding him. All he could conjure was the image of Eicko's contorted face, those white flames pouring out of the crevice. If it hadn't been for his brother, Brade never would have made it this far. The workers stared at each other, waiting awkwardly.

"Not many of you know how this all began," Brade finally said. "Or to whom we all owe this incredible success. Eighteen years ago, my brother discovered the source of the *black air*, right here, where the *bore* you all helped build stands today. My brother Eicko always sought a great adventure. That search led him to find the *black air*." Brade stared into the darkness of the well. "Unfortunately, his life was ended before he could realize what that discovery meant. But his death was not in vain. His death showed me Albadone's potential." Brade realized his eyes were welling up with tears. He wiped his face. "Today we have made a new discovery: *black water*. As you can see, it is much easier to transport than the *black air*, but it is made of the same stuff. Today, we pave the way for a new Albadone. Tomorrow, Albadone shall be brighter than the stars!"

Cheers shook the worksite. Brade couldn't help but smile, tears running freely into his dark beard. As a youth, Brade never allowed himself to mourn his twin's death, instead, burying himself into his work, struggling to give meaning to Eicko's passing. Today, finally, he felt that he had found that meaning. His tears were both in mourning and celebration. Their release left him feeling whole.

Brade wiped his face, composing himself. He raised a hand, and the cheers died gradually. "In recognition of a job well done, I invite you all to *The Rat's Nest* for drinks and merriment." If the cheers were loud before, now they were explosive. Soon, the worksite was cleared of all the workers except for the guards—Brade promised them a paid day off that they could take at their will. It wasn't often that he saw the worksite so empty. He reflected on all his hard work, all that time spent apart from his wife and children. He looked up at the *bore*: the large wooden structure towered over all—at that moment, Brade felt just as tall. A sudden calm washed over him, and he held onto it.

Other than the guards, Brade was the last man at the site—or so he thought. Yona gave Brade a pat on the back that made his bones ring, startling him out of his calm. "Nice speech there," the burly man said. "I must say, I wish I shared your optimistic vision of the future."

Brade smirked. "Always the pessimist."

"I've been alive long enough to never trust a good thing. So much is happening in Albadone so quickly... Woodsfolk aren't known for their adaptability."

"That may very well be," Brade chuckled. "But I know what I'm doing. This..." he gestured to Yona's stained body, "*black water* could be what sets Albadone apart from the rest. Do you know why the townsfolk are richer than we are, both in wealth and in health?" Brade didn't wait for a reply. "It's because they embrace change. They don't blindly follow tradition and lore as we do. They make informed decisions. And that's what has allowed them to build great cities like Vizen. They adapt."

"Adapt, sure," Yona said, pensively. "But do you know what stood there, three hundred years ago, where Vizen stands now?"

Brade rolled his eyes. "The trees."

"A forest of *wishing* trees," Yona corrected.

"There's no actual historical evidence of such a forest ever existing."

"Whether they were wishing trees or not, Vizen stands now where Albadone once reached. Sure, the townsfolk are inclined to adapt, but there is no world in which progress can happen without destruction."

"What are you trying to say?"

Yona tugged on his beard—no doubt the cause of its stringiness. "Only that progress always comes at a cost. The pessimist in me dreads that it is one we cannot afford. But what am I but a simple miner working to put food on his family's table?"

Brade walked with Yona all the way to *The Rat's Nest* in Pevine. It was a brisk hour's walk and the sun was beginning its descent as they neared the town. In the tavern, the young barmaid, Alanda, was serving all the workers with a smile, her baby, Olmer, wrapped in a bundle around her chest. To see Alanda moving so quickly and serving drinks with a smile while also tending to her child was a testament to the young woman's ability. She reminded Brade of how his wife, Yolta, had cared for their baby Elger and their two older boys that were so much like him and Eicko. His work kept him away from them more often than not. At times, he had to convince himself, and, in particular, his wife, that it would all be worth it in the end. Brade decided to retire after one drink, much to the protests of the workers. He handed Alanda a pouch full of pieces—his 'purse in Vizen' wouldn't mind the splurge, especially not after finding out about their discovery. "This should cover them for the rest of the night." Brade hurried out the door as the protests behind him turned to cheers.

Night had descended, the moon looming brightly in the dark sky. The year had been much cooler than usual—the Spring seemed reluctant to break the pattern. Brade lifted his hood against the chill and tinkered with his lantern prototype as he made his way home. It was a long walk, and, as of late, he had made it even longer by taking a detour route home to avoid any proximity to Mother Adriel's cabin. The enchantress lived too close for comfort, in Brade's opinion. Once his prototype was operational, Brade planned on moving his family to Pevine. He hadn't run the idea by Yolta yet, but he was sure she'd agree. His home stood in a small clearing: unlike their neighbors' homes it was built with brick and stone—Yolta had thought it strange, but Brade was insistent that it would hold up and maintain heat much better than thatch and wood. That Winter, Yolta had been grateful for it. The alluring orange glow of the hearth beckoned Brade inside.

As soon as Brade opened the door, Hammen and Toller crashed against him in a wave of youthful energy, hugging their father tightly. "Papa!" they exclaimed in unison.

"What did you do?" Brade deadpanned. His boys were only ever this eager to greet him at the door if they had gotten in trouble with their mother.

"Toller won't stop teaching Hammen curse words," Yolta stated, entering the living space through the bedroom door. "And where he learned them in the first place still eludes me."

"Which one was it this time?" Brade asked Toller with a grin.

"Brade!" Yolta swatted at her husband before their son could answer.

Brade kissed his sons' heads. "Listen to your mother. If I hear that you've cursed again, I'll make you chop so much wood you'll be pulling splinters from your hands for weeks."

The boys giggled and ran off. "Quiet!" Yolta shushed, attempting to keep a level voice. "I just put the babe to sleep." The boys stopped running and returned to their wooden horses—Brade had built the small figures with movable joints he had designed himself; it brought him an indescribable joy to watch his sons play with them. "How was today?" Yolta asked, giving Brade a warm kiss on the cheek.

Brade scooped her into the air, his excitement bursting from him like the *black water* had from the pump. "We did it, my love. Everything I worked so hard for has come to fruition." He told his wife about the discovery of the *black water* and of how easy it would be to store it. Soon, even his children stopped playing to listen—their eyes wide. "The possibilities are endless. Imagine a hearth that never dies. Lanterns that need not be lit because they never go out."

"That's wonderful," Yolta hugged him tightly. "Perhaps now you'll be able to spend a bit more time with us here. You're dearly missed, as you most likely can tell. We can even have a big dinner soon to celebrate, like tomorrow!" Yolta's eyes were bright with planning, "I'll roast a boar. Invite some friends, perhaps even Mother Adriel—"

"Tomorrow is no good," Brade interrupted. His smile had vanished quickly upon hearing the enchantress's name. "I'll be at the site. There's still a good deal of work to be done."

"Oh, all right then," Yolta turned to walk away. Brade grabbed her wrist, firmly but not forcefully, and she turned to face him.

"Yolta, I am so close," he said fervently. "Soon I will appoint a replacement foreman to oversee the worksite, and then I'll be home every day." Yolta expression remained sullen. "What do you want me to do, abandon my workers?"

Yolta seemed to have something to say hanging on the tip of her tongue, but she held back. Instead, she put on a smile. "It's just... you've been saying you're so close for so long. First, it was the *bore*, then the *black air*, now this *water*," she sighed. "What will keep you from us next?"

A baby's wail sounded from the bedroom. Yolta turned and headed in, followed by Brade a few paces behind. The walls of the bedroom were adorned with woven tapestries and painted plates that had been passed down to them from Yolta's family. Unlike many of their neighbors, who slept on cots and mats, they had a townsfolk bed—Brade had it brought in from Vizen. Yolta often joked that Brade was a townsman in disguise—there was some truth to that; at times he barely felt like he belonged among other woodsfolk.

The child's face was red and wrinkled as a prune, his cries filling the room. Yolta picked him up, shushing gently. She unfastened her blouse and released a breast, allowing baby Elger to suckle, placating his cries. Brade stood at the threshold watching them in awe. Elger's hair had started to grow, dark and thick like his. Everything he worked on was for them. All of his successes were theirs too. How could he make them understand?

"One thing I've always loved about you is your spirit," Yolta said, almost in a whisper. "You know what you want, and you work hard for it. For that, I do not fault you. But your sons... They're good boys, but, True One, they can be such a handful. They need their father, and I need more help. There's so much that needs to be done here."

"I'm so close, Yolta. So close."

"I know. You've already said so."

Brade stood at the door for a few more moments, then turned and headed back into the living area. Toller stood by the red-hot hearth, holding his wooden horse over the flames as Hammen watched nearby. Eicko's face flashed in his mind and then was lost in a burst of white fire. Brade realized he had forcefully grabbed the horse from Toller's hand and smacked the boy across his face. Toller stood dumbfounded, his hand on his reddening cheek. Tears began to form in his eyes, but he held them back. Brade returned the wooden horse to him.

"What did I tell you about playing with fire?" Brade said, keeping his voice low. "I better not see you do anything like that ever again, understood?"

"Yes, Papa," Toller said with a sniff.

Brade turned to Hammen. The younger child's cheeks were soaked in tears. "You too."

"Y-yes, Papa," the boy choked out.

"Now go to your room. It's time for bed." The two boys hurried off to their room without a word. This wasn't how Brade had wanted the evening to end. The quiet calm of the house felt heavy now. Yolta was right. These boys needed their father. But he was so close. So close.

XII.

A Darkness So Dim

The ending of the prior night's conversation with Yolta had left a sour taste in Brade's mouth. He also disliked sending his sons to bed after having yelled at them. They hadn't given him a choice. But they were children, and children were quick to forgive. The sun seemed slow to rise that morning, yet the birds were already up and chirping away as Brade slipped out of the house, his still nonfunctional lantern in hand—hopefully, he would find time today to tinker with it. It was earlier than when he usually left for the worksite, but with luck, an early day meant an early return home.

The path to the worksite was long but clear. Woodsfolk had never bothered with developing roads, instead priding themselves on knowing how to navigate the woods without the need for landmarks to show them the way. The two roads that crossed Albadone were the *Yellow Road* and the *Red Road*, both commissioned by the Talessi royal family of Vizen two decades earlier. The *Yellow Road* was constructed as a way to easily transport merchandise by cart from Vizen to the northern city of Perimat, while the *Red Road* ran eastward, towards Rondhill and beyond. The woodsfolk had protested the building of the roads since many trees had to be felled to make way for them. Perhaps there was some truth in what Yona had said. *Progress comes at a cost.*

The guards stood at the perimeter of the worksite—most of them alert, he was happy to notice. The guard had changed halfway through the night to allow the ones from the previous day to rest. They weren't armed beyond batons—Brade didn't want them to hurt anyone, only to dissuade any folk from causing trouble.

"Anything to report?" he asked a guard with a flat nose that must have seen more than one punch in its past—he was new, so Brade hadn't memorized his name yet.

"Nay, sir," the guard replied. "Only a few cries in the night."

"Cries?" Brade asked. "What do you mean?"

"Animals, sir. Perhaps a large bird of prey shrieking while nesting. We've heard the sounds before in the past weeks, but from a distance. These sounded much closer, not even a few yards away."

Brade smirked at the guard. "Are they a cause for concern, these birds?"

"No, sir, just loud is all."

"Carry on," Brade said, patting the guard on the shoulder.

Next, he inspected the barrels—today was the day they would finally be put to use. They had one hundred of the wooden barrels and twenty-three steel ones and counting. He would have his workers focus on the production of the wooden barrels from now on, as they were faster and cheaper to produce, and the discovery of *black water* had renewed their utility. Brade assumed that this *black water* had the same properties as the *black air*, but he needed to be sure. Four barrels were stacked near the pump and labeled 'Full'. He knew a man in Pevine, a townsfolk named

Kelmer, who was an accomplished chemist. Brade would have one of these barrels sent to him and examined.

He wasn't at all surprised to see Yona arrive at the worksite well before anyone else—the man truly held the mining operation together, having had years of experience in his youth digging for ore in the Womb of the World. Soon after, as daylight, at last, brightened the woods with its golden light, the worksite began to buzz with activity. The stocky mule cart driver he had hired to transport supplies back and forth from the site to Pevine, arrived slightly later than everyone else. His cart was full of food supplies for the day—potatoes, carrots, beets, and several chickens—and a large wooden casket.

"What's in there?" Brade asked the driver as the man parked his mule cart at the edge of the worksite.

"Wine, master Brade," the man said, his chins bouncing as he spoke.

Brade recoiled with a start. As the Winter had grown heavier and heavier, wine had become harder to come by. Many of the nearby vineyards had not recovered their fruit, and the few barrels that could be found came from Sol Forne, which were much too expensive. But drink was a part of work—that was the woodsman in him—so he had swapped the wine for ale, at least until the cost of wine returned to a reasonable rate with the Summer harvest.

"Where did you come by this wine?" Brade asked, as four men lifted the cask off the cart and rolled it away towards the mess tent.

The driver seemed reluctant to say. "Well, sir, last night I had quite a few drinks at the *Nest* after all the workers left for their homes." He was fidgeting with the mule's bridle. "I may have let slip of your discovery to one Jecobe Sandar, a merchant headed to Vizen from Rondhill. This Sandar fellow then gave me this cask of good Sol Forne as a sign of goodwill, in hopes that you would consider, perhaps, selling a barrel or two of *black water* to him." Before Brade could say a word, the driver added, "Master Brade, could you find it within yourself to forgive me? I don't drink ale very often, and I found myself with a light head and a loose tongue. I didn't mean anything by it, and the offer of wine for the worksite seemed too good to pass."

Brade's 'purse in Vizen' would not appreciate word of the discovery spreading. A person who took measures to ensure that their identity was secret, operating exclusively through missives and envoys, would not be too happy to have their investment made public. Brade's mouth soured at first, but the pitiful expression on the driver's face made him almost chuckle. "I'll speak with this Sandar fellow, to ensure word doesn't get out any further. In the meanwhile, I need you to take one barrel of *black water* to Pevine. Find Kelmer, the chemist, and tell him I sent you. He'll know what to do."

"Aye, sir." The driver seemed to have expected a reprimand or punishment. Brade took slight offense—he could be hard with his workers at times, but he never thought of himself as cruel or unjust.

As the driver turned to ask for assistance with the barrels, Brade added, "And lay off the ale for a while," with a brief smirk.

Ensuring that the worksite was operating as it should had taken up most of Brade's day when he had first hired men to build the *bore*. As the seasons passed, however, he found himself having to do less and less—the workers knew what they were supposed to be doing and where they needed to be. There were times, especially recently, that Brade felt entirely redundant—he would not have had it any other way. After all, a worksite that operated well, without needing to be tended to was a successful one.

Brade surveyed the worksite. At the far edge, the lumber yard was the busiest it had been since the operation began. Lumbermen stacked logs in a neat pile, as woodworkers fashioned them into planks; the planks were then given to the barrel makers who bundled them together with iron hoops produced by the blacksmiths. The wheel on the *bore* was being turned by a strong worker—Brade would have to devise a way to automate that process—and the pump was spewing the *black water* into barrels. In the mineshaft below the well, craftsmen had been instructed to rebuild the *sifter* so that it could pump the *water* more effectively. As some miners continued digging, Yona had instructed several others to focus on maintaining the pipes.

Nothing about the site needed tending to this very moment so Brade contentedly focused on his lantern. He sat near the mess tent as the cook, Yallot—*who makes me eat a lot*—stripped the meat off a goat carcass nearby. Brade lifted the glass chimney, revealing the wool mesh within the lantern. Under the mesh was a canister designed to be filled with *black air*. Brade would have to rethink his design now that the lantern would be fueled by a liquid. Perhaps a wick would do the trick.

A commotion at the other side of the worksite distracted Brade from his lantern. Workers had gathered around something, some of them yelling and calling out for help. A familiar voice was whimpering. Brade had to push his way through the onlookers—whatever had happened stole their attention enough that they didn't part for him as they usually did. The flat-nosed guard was carrying the driver through the crowd as he yelled, "Make way!" The driver's leg was bloody and mangled, dangling horridly as if still attached by a meager thread. Some of the workers turned and emptied their stomachs at the sight.

"True One!" Brade exclaimed, a tremor in his voice betraying an attempt at stoicism. "What happened?"

"I heard yells in the woods, sir," the guard explained. "I ran out there and found him like this. His mule was gone, ripped from the cart."

"Somebody, go to town and bring back a healer!" Brade barked the order to no one in particular. The guard laid the driver on the ground. The man was shivering in pain, his face pale and sweaty. Brade kneeled in front of him, holding the man's head between his hands—it felt feverish. "What happened?"

The driver struggled to form words. "A b-b-b-b," he stuttered in a whisper. Brade put his ear to the man's mouth to get a better listen. "A b-b-beas-s-s-t."

"A beast?" Brade asked. "What sort of beast?"

The driver's trembling turned into convulsions and then a seizure. His eyes went white as they rolled back. "Stay with me... *you.*" Brade realized just then that he couldn't recall the driver's name—why couldn't he remember his name?

A *shriek* like that of an eagle, but much louder, filled the air. The worksite went quiet. Brade lifted his head and looked out at the edge of the woods. Mother Adriel stood there, watching him from a distance, her hood up over her eyes. What was the enchantress doing there? Did she have anything to do with this?

"Master Brade." Brade looked up at the flat-nosed guard who had called him. The guard—True One, he needed to learn his name—nodded towards the driver. Only then did Brade realize that the man's head was limp in his hands. The driver had died. And Brade couldn't even recall his name. He carefully set the man's head on the ground and turned his gaze back to the edge of the woods: the enchantress was nowhere to be seen.

"Someone cover him up. And you," Brade pointed at the flat-nosed guard, "watch him until the healer arrives."

The guard nodded sullenly. "Aye, sir."

"What's your name, son?" Brade asked the man.

"It's Stecklass, sir."

Brade nodded at the young guard. *Stecklass—who saw the nameless driver pass.*

Realizing his hands were covered in the driver's blood, Brade made his way to the wash station, where the miners cleaned up after a long day's work. He dipped his hands in the lukewarm water sitting in the basin and scrubbed the blood off. *A beast*, the driver had said. *Greatwolves* were known for prowling the woods, but they usually avoided areas where lots of folk gathered. And besides, Spring was their mating season. Perhaps a lone *greatwolf* had strayed from the pack—that had to be it.

Mother Adriel's words entered his thoughts, unbidden as they were unwelcome. *Beneath Albadone lies its lifeblood, and the* melk *have returned to defend it.* He splashed his face quickly, hoping to rinse away the thoughts of the enchantress—and of *melk*. It must have been a *greatwolf.*

The worksite struggled to regain its previous pace—the men kept glancing at the driver's body, now covered by a slowly bloodying blanket. It took several hours for a chemist to arrive. Brade didn't care much for Chemist Ovan. The man was hairless and pink like a baby mole and was always licking his cracked lips and sniffing. Stecklass appeared uncomfortable as he escorted the chemist to the body—and not entirely because of the body, Brade suspected. Chemist Ovan uncovered the driver and observed him closely, covering his nose with a white handkerchief that smelled faintly of mint.

"My apologies I couldn't arrive sooner," Chemist Ovan said upon seeing Brade approach. "Was he dead when you found him?"

"His leg was mangled when I brought him here," Stecklass said. "He died soon after I laid him down."

"I see," the chemist said, licking his dry lips. He pulled a small metal prodder from his belt and poked the wound—even Stecklass had to look away. "Any idea how it happened?"

"No, sir," the guard said.

Chemist Ovan turned to Brade, who shook his head in agreement with the guard. "It's quite a bite. Much larger than that of a *greatwolf* or any other sort of *woodsbeast*. No tooth marks either, which is quite peculiar." The chemist stood and faced Brade. "I'd keep an eye out if I were you. I noticed your guards only carry batons. Perhaps it's time to arm them? Some bows or spears might do the trick."

"Couldn't hurt," Brade agreed.

The chemist wiped the bloody prodder with the handkerchief and returned it to his belt. He turned his attention to the *bore*. "I may have heard of a discovery of yours from a merchant in Pevine. Some sort of *black water*." Brade sighed deeply—this strange man seemed to draw pleasure from the discomfort of those around him. "The stuff may have some medicinal value. If I might suggest a partnership, there could be quite a bit of pieces in it for the both of us. Of course, I would require some of the material first, to examine its properties."

The chemist was pushing it, but Brade had to admit he had a point. Perhaps using the *black water* as fuel was simply one of its many possible uses. But the *water* wasn't his to give. "I'm but a foreman," Brade said through a forced smile. "I'll bring up your suggestion to my employer and, if he agrees to it, you'll receive a missive. In the meantime, I'd appreciate your discretion in the matter."

The chemist dry-washed his hands and smiled. His yellowed teeth made his face seem even more sinister. "But of course," he said. "As for the body, I can take that off your hands. Any idea if he had family or anyone close?"

Brade felt a tightness in his chest. "I do not."

"No worries, I'll work something out.' Helped by two workers, the chemist loaded the body on the back of a mule cart parked at the edge of the woods. Once it was secured and the chemist took his seat at the front, the driver flicked the reins, and the mule dragged the cart into the woods.

The workday carried on as if nothing had happened. Brade told Stecklass he was free to head home if he wished. The guard turned down his offer—it appeared he was wary of traveling the woods alone; who could blame him? Standing atop a pile of planks with the workers encircling him, Brade addressed the worksite. He explained that no one was to leave without at least two others with them. The workers nodded in agreement. Brade's announcement would have assured them, had the end of his speech not been punctuated by a piercing *shriek* that emanated from the woods. The workers flinched and instinctively huddled together.

"No need to worry," Brade assured them, struggling to keep a level voice. "I'm sure that whatever that is—" He hadn't even finished his sentence when another *shriek* sounded from a different direction, this one much closer. Then another *shriek* replied elsewhere. And another.

Brade swallowed the bile at the back of his throat. A silent panic descended on the worksite—Brade had to think quickly. "Perhaps," he called out, regaining the workers' attention—but only partially. "Perhaps we've done enough work for a day. Clean up your stations and head home. And don't worry, you will all be compensated as if you had finished the workday." That seemed to put the men somewhat at ease. Anxiously, they returned to their stations and cleared them. Within the hour, they had all left for their homes.

Brade inspected the vacant worksite—its stillness sent shivers running down his neck. He collected his prototype lantern and turned to the woods. A tight grip on his shoulder halted him. "What do you think you're doing?" Yona asked.

"I'm headed home," Brade answered.

"Didn't you say no one was to leave alone?"

Brade smiled at the man. "Always the pessimist. I'll be all right. What about you? Are you headed home as well?"

"Me? No. Us miners still have a lot of work to see to. It seems we've struck another shaft that's full of the stuff. And besides, whatever is in those woods is more likely to get you than reach us down there." Brade nodded and turned his gaze to the woods—the impenetrable trees swaying in the gentle breeze. "What do you think it was that did that?" Yona asked.

Brade halted. The last thing he wanted to do was ponder that question. "I don't know."

"Keep safe," Yona said, his voice surprisingly somber.

Brade looked at the man—up close, his ugliness was somewhat charming. "I will," he replied, and with that, he entered the woods.

Brade once again took the detour path, doing his best to circumvent the enchantress's cabin. He had told the woman to stay away from the worksite, yet time after time she ignored him. Could she have had something to do with today's accident? Impossible. While he disliked Mother Adriel very much, he just couldn't see the young woman doing something of that sort.

A *shriek* broke him from his contemplation with a start. The *shrieking* continued for some time, loud and uninterrupted, bouncing off the trees, coming from one thousand directions at the same time. Another *shriek* came as an answer, then another. Eventually, the woods were inundated with them, all surrounding him. Brade ran as fast as he could through the forest.

Visions of Eicko engulfed by white flames fogged his mind. He focused on his family, Yolta, Hammen, Toller, and baby Elger—he had to reach them quickly, make sure they were safe. The *shrieks* sounded closer, almost as if they came from the dark trees immediately around him. Had the forest always been this thick? It felt as if it was trying to swallow him.

By the time Brade reached the clearing where his home stood, darkness had descended. The *shrieks* had grown so loud and continuous that he couldn't be sure he wasn't simply imagining them. As he ran into the clearing, his foot caught onto a root—it almost felt as if the root had grabbed him—and he tripped, falling to the ground. He felt his way through the blackness, his hand touching a strange depression formed in the dirt: a four-toed track, but bigger than that of a *greatwolf*. Brade could now see that the clearing was covered in those tracks—several sets from multiple beasts. That's when Brade finally noticed that the door to his home had been torn off its hinges, laying in two several feet away.

A beast, the driver had said.

"No..." The whisper was a prayer. He leapt up and ran to the door. He stopped at the threshold and called out, "Yolta?"

No one answered.

Brade's heart was a fat toad jumping in his chest. His breath felt as thick and sticky as the *black water*. He took a step into the dark house—a few smoking red embers remained in the hearth—and called out again. "Yolta? Toller? Hammen?" No one answered.

The wooden floor was splintered in every direction where deep claw marks ran across it. The table he had built years earlier sat overturned and smashed. There was no sign of his family. He slowly headed for the bedroom, a cold dread setting in. A small wooden horse lay on the busted floor in front of the doorway. It took one peek into the room for the blood to drain from his face. His family lay in there. Broken.

Before he knew it, his head hit the floor, and the light drained from the world.

XIII.

A LIGHT THAT NEVER DIES

"Eicko!?" Brade cried out. The white flame streamed out of the chasm—its suddenness hadn't allowed Brade any time to process. His eyebrows were singed, as were the tips of his hair, but he paid them no mind. "Eicko?" he called out again, this time more faintly, no longer expecting a reply. He wasn't sure how long he stood there, watching those flames—it could have been moments—or hours. Eventually, Brade placed the firestarter in his pocket and returned home.

When his parents asked where his twin was, he had no answer to give other than, "He's gone," which brought an onslaught of more questions that he couldn't bring himself to answer. In time, he resigned and simply said, "I don't know where he is," with a dismissive shrug.

It was as if his family had descended into the chasm with Eicko—into a darkness so dim. He never told his parents the truth about what happened that day. The birth of twins was seen as a blessing in Albadone but losing one twin was believed to be akin to a curse—the True One had entrusted them with a blessing, and they had failed Him. What surprised Brade the most was his father's reaction. He was already a silent man, speaking only when he must. Eicko's death made the man turn further inward. He focused entirely on his work, seemingly giving up on fathering altogether. Brade never faulted him for that, but he missed his father often—hardness and all.

He returned to the chasm every day after the incident, watching as the flames continued to pour upwards, like a waterfall cascading into the sky. Others had begun to visit there as well, their eyes wide with awe, as if witnessing a miracle. When the flames finally subsided several days later, after a heavy rainstorm, Brade peeked into the chasm. The still blackness below gripped at his chest with an icy claw. He realized he had been hoping Eicko would crawl out wearing one of his toothy grins. His twin would shove his shoulder and tease him, *"Why are you always so scared?"* Brade imagined him saying.

But the only thing in the chasm was that impenetrable blackness. For a long time after that, Brade feared the darkness of their bedroom—*his* bedroom—at night, feared closing his eyes.

❦ ❦ ❦ ❦

Brade's eyes opened. Darkness still surrounded him—suffocating. A dull throbbing at his temple reminded him that he had fallen. Shards of glass where the prototype lantern had crashed were scattered about the busted floorboards. He remained laying down, unmoving, for what seemed like a brief eternity. Why had he been on the floor again?

A *shriek* emanating from the woods brought him to his feet. He turned his head to the open bedroom door. The darkness inside that room seemed thicker and deeper than the one that currently enveloped him. A cold shiver crept down his neck and collected in his chest. Brade wept bitterly at the recollection that his family was gone—and with them all his dreams. He had spent his life so focused on the future but, without them, there wasn't one. How could he have done this to them?

"If you don't cease your digging right now, they will find you and they will kill you and every other man, woman, and child that inhabits these woods."

The enchantress' words gnawed at the back of his mind like termites in wood. Mother Adriel had warned him again and again that this would happen, and he had repeatedly ignored her. This was all his fault. Brade hit the wall with a weak fist. How many other woodsfolk had he sentenced to die because of his work? *Work*—the word was acid. But perhaps there was still something he could do to stop it.

His gaze settled on the hearth where the last two embers were dying to gray—and a thought was born. If the *bore* was the cause of this, then the *bore* must be destroyed. It shocked him how easily the idea came to him. Shouldn't having to destroy his life's work be harder to stomach? Guilt was a hot poker prodding his ribs. *My family was my life's work.*

Once outside, a part of him wanted to turn back, to look one last time at the home he had built for his family. But he couldn't bring himself to do so. Several *shrieks* sounded through the woods: a reminder of his mission. He ran through the darkness of Albadone towards the worksite. He had taken this road so many times, it felt like second nature—even the treacherous darkness couldn't slow him down. However, the forest itself seemed to want to stop him. The trees breathed and moved; their roots gnarled and slithered as if trying to catch him in their vengeful snares.

When he finally reached the worksite, he ignored his body's screams for respite and his lungs begging for air. He made his way past a sleeping guard posted at the edge of the forest—seeing that would have irritated him before—and headed for the *bore*. At the pump, two workers were filling a barrel with the *black water*. He couldn't believe Yona and his crew had stayed so late—or perhaps it wasn't so late; Brade's sense of time had turned upside-down: it could be just before dawn for all he knew.

Yona stood by the well, looking out into the swaying darkness of the woods as the *shrieking* surrounded them. Brade ran up to the man, finally stopping to catch his breath.

"Brade?" Yona inquired, unsure that he was seeing right. "I thought you turned in for the night." Brade was about to reply when a nearby *shriek* cut him off. Yona put his hand on the foreman's shoulder, only now getting a good look at his gaunt face and sunken eyes. "Brade... is everything all right, friend?"

Brade swallowed, feeling icy dread scrape his lungs. "We must stop," was all he could force out between heavy breaths.

"Stop what?" Yona asked, calmly.

Brade looked over at the pump—the workers had stopped pumping the *black water*, their eyes on him now. "We have to stop!" Brade yelled in their direction, doing his best to make it sound like an order and not the ravings of a madman. Shrugging out of Yona's hold, Brade headed for the pump. The two workers stepped aside, and Brade pushed the barrel over, spilling the *black water* onto the ground.

Yona grabbed Brade's arm firmly and yanked him away from the downed barrel. "What are you doing?" Yona asked, his expression somewhere between anger, confusion, and concern. "Have you gone mad?"

Brade shoved Yona aside and walked to the outer circle of the worksite, towards a stump with an ax buried into it. He pulled the ax out of the stump with some effort and then faced the *bore*. When Yona realized what was about to happen, he quickly grabbed Brade's arm.

"Take the ax away from him!" Yona cried out to the two workers, who joined him in tackling Brade.

"You don't understand!" Brade thrashed, hysterically now—the *shrieks* coming from the dark edge of the woods matched him in volume. When the ax was removed from his hand, the workers relaxed their hold on him. Yona let go of Brade as well, as he had seemingly calmed down. But before anyone could do anything, Brade made for the *bore* like a feral beast, attempting to dismantle it by hand. It was a futile and pathetic sight, Brade knew, but his mind was set on destroying the cursed thing.

"True One! He's lost his damned mind!" Yona exclaimed in shock. Once more, Yona restrained Brade, this time with a thick arm around the crazed foreman's neck. "Stay still!" Yona yelled as Brade floundered, kicking in the other man's grasp.

"Let me go!" Brade's voice was hoarse with exasperation.

"Not until you tell me what has gotten into you."

The image of his family scattered across the bedroom flashed before his eyes. His strength drained from him. He fell limply into Yona's arms, sobbing bitterly. "They're dead... they're all dead..." Each word was a knife to the chest.

"Who is dead?" Yona asked, concern softening his tone.

"Yolta... the kids... True One, even the baby..."

"Brade, what are you saying?"

"She was right. The damned enchantress was right. What we're doing here has unleashed an evil upon this land, and we all bear the curse. We must tear it all down before it spreads, and they kill us all." Several echoing *shrieks* punctuated the statement.

Yona let go of Brade, allowing him to fall softly to his knees. "What does any of this have to do with us? With our work?"

"The True One made the *melk* to guard the forest," Brade said, his gaze trained on the dark tree line. He could swear he saw something moving out there—something big. "And now the *melk* have returned to punish us all."

"Are you hearing yourself?" A flash of anger colored Yona's voice. "This is madness."

Brade turned to Yona—the man's face held far less rage than his voice had. Was that fear that touched his eyes?

"Are you not listening?" Brade begged. "We have to dismantle all of this before they punish you too and all of Albadone—as they did with me."

The worker wielding the ax stepped beside Yona—Brade couldn't make out who the man was in the dark. "Should we have a guard escort him home?" the worker asked Yona.

Brade's head pulsed with red heat. "We're wasting time!" he bellowed. A scream echoed from the edge of the worksite. They all faced that direction as the screams were overtaken by monstrous *shrieks*. Brade knew they wouldn't have much longer.

"What was that?"

"They're here," Brade said, his sobs turning to manic laughter. "We're too late. Leave this cursed place while you still have the chance."

Heavy footsteps neared at a gallop. The upper half of the ax-wielding worker was ripped from him and dragged away by a massive shadow. The beast was at least three times bigger than the largest *greatwolf* Brade had ever seen. The other worker bolted into the darkness.

Yona lifted Brade by his arm. "We have to get out of here!" the ugly man exclaimed.

Brade lunged out of Yona's hold. "I must stay. Save yourself."

Yona shook his head then disappeared into the night. A *shriek* emanated from close enough that Brade could feel the air shift around him. With no time to waste, he made for the well. Debris fell onto the ground, as the sound of crunching wood came from above. Brade looked up: a large, wingless, bird-like creature, its feathers flashing silver, was shredding the top of the *bore* with its razor-sharp talons and blood-drenched beak. The creature turned and locked him in its gaze—he was its prey. It *shrieked* at him and clamored down the side of the *bore* towards him. Brade instinctively took a few steps back. Before he could stop himself, he felt the emptiness behind him as he fell into the dark well.

The air was sucked out of him as he landed on his back with a dull thud. He didn't feel any pain, only the cold. His head was a brick and his legs hollow and wooden. Thick warm blood made its way up his throat and into his mouth. Miners surrounded him—their voices filled with concern, but their words sounded jumbled and nonsensical to Brade. At the mouth of the well above, the beast's black eyes peered in. A *shriek* echoed through the mineshaft walls—piercing and monstrous. As the creature descended into the well, its talons grabbing onto the rocky walls, the miners scrambled about fearfully. They stood no chance.

The chaos around Brade felt like a hazy half-remembered dream, the *shrieks* of the beast intertwining with the screams of the miners into a cacophonous melody. The dark smell of blood mixed with that of the *black air* resulted in a putrid and sickly scent. Brade attempted to lift his head, but it felt heavy and numb. He could feel the life slowly drain away from him like water slipping between fingers—but he held onto it dearly.

He saw a miner reach for the rope ladder, attempting an escape. The beast—a *melk*, he was sure of it now—grabbed the miner in its beak and tore him in half with ease, as if he were made of fresh butter. Half of the miner cascaded onto the shaft floor in a gory display. The *melk* wasn't here to eat—purely to destroy.

The white flames that had engulfed Eicko now burned through Brade's memory. He had dreamed of illuminating Albadone with flames that would never go out, dispelling the darkness from the woods and his life, forever—he smiled at the irony. He reached into his pocket where he had kept the firestarter ever since that day so many Springs ago. The pain in his broken leg was someone else's pain. When his fingers finally found the firestarter, the metal instrument was heavy in his weak hand.

The *melk* had finally realized that he was the only person still alive in the shaft. Its pitch-black eyes fixed on him as it approached. With what strength he had left, Brade squeezed the firestarter—unlike when he was a boy, the sparks flew out on the first try. The white flames arrived with beastly fury, engulfing him, the *melk*, and the mineshaft in its jaws. Brade could see his family in the light—Yolta, Hammen, Toller, baby Elger, and Eicko—all smiling at him. Finally, the world didn't seem so dark anymore.

※ ※ ※ ※

The enchantress stood on Chanter's Hill, watching the dark woods below. She couldn't remember the last time she had made the journey there as it was a long and arduous hike from her cabin. Yet, she felt a memory of trekking up the hill recently flicker at the rear of her mind—she was searching for mushrooms, she thought. She touched the *melk* feather adorning her hair—Adriel, the girl she had taken, had given it to her as a gift. But what had her previous name been? Olla, she thought, but she couldn't be sure. How many times had she performed *Transference*? How many more would it take for her to live long enough to finish her mission? Considering the recent happenings, probably longer than she'd like.

She looked out over the moonlit forest—the sight brought her a strange sort of comfort, but she knew it wouldn't last long. Brade, that fool, had been too late in doing anything about that hideous structure he was building. The *melk* had returned to Albadone in full force and would soon begin their destruction. The beasts were driven by two things: the Cycle of Nature would be equalized and the lifeblood of Albadone protected.

Mother Adriel had spent several months preparing for this eventuality. She had traveled into Pevine more times than she would have liked to hire drivers and movers to collect her belongings from her shabby cabin and move them into a cave she had claimed atop the Womb of the World.

"Are you leaving Albadone, Mother?" a mover asked her.

"Temporarily," she answered. *"The Womb of the World will be the only safe haven for the next few seasons. I suggest you and those you love move near the mountain as well if you have any care for your lives."*

She hoped the mover took her suggestion to heart, although she doubted it. These townsfolk cared about comfort above most else—why do anything to inconvenience their little lives? Unlike them, she had never much cared for comfort. Her old cabin was proof of that—however, as of late, she could barely stand being in that shabby old place.

Shrieking filled the forest from every direction, confirmation that all of her warnings would come to a head tonight. Blood would be spilled, lives lost. And for what? Progress, Brade had told her. Hubris was more like it.

She saw the pale flames erupt out of the wooden structure before she heard the cacophonous explosion that followed. Then the hot air reached her in waves. The flames were a hand that greedily reached for the woods, touching everything in sight. The *shrieking* came to a sudden halt. Another eruption of fire, this time several miles away, created a wall of flames that loomed over the canopy. Then elsewhere, near Pevine, another tower of fire. The *lifeblood* of Albadone had ignited. Nothing would stop its destruction now.

Mother Adriel watched in awe as the forest—*her* forest—was engulfed in flames. If this was the cost the True One had set, then so be it. But the enchantress couldn't help the tears of mourning that ran down her face at the sight. This punishment would set her back decades. How many more apprentices was it going to take for her to regain what she had lost? *It will take what it takes.*

Without wasting time, Mother Adriel retreated to her cave in the Womb *of the World*. As the fire swept through the woods, the enchantress felt all of it through her connection to the Cycle. Hot flashes of pain shot through her body day and night. She felt weak and feverish. The pain grew, leaving her convulsing from it, and just when she thought she could no longer take it, ten days later, it began to rain.

"True One be praised," she exclaimed, as the rain soothed the flames.

It took three days for the rain to extinguish the fires, and three more to cool the remaining embers. What remained of Albadone was a mere shadow of what had been. The verdant Spring had become a graying corpse. It would take a long time to recuperate, years even, but there was no sense in waiting.

It's time I return to work.

SUMMER:
A Mother

XIV.

Scars

One week had passed since the last fires died down, or at least, that's what the traveling merchant pushing a cart full of pitiful wares had told Ashe. Spring—if it could be called that—had fizzled out into a mild Summer. The fires had left an ominous gray fog that enveloped the forest of Albadone like a curse. On a few rare days, a light breeze from the distant western ocean would blow in like a gentle kiss and the fog would lift, just slightly, only to return immediately. The gray had become a fixture of the woods.

Skeletal trees waved ghoulishly as Ashe made her way through what remained of the forest. Two months ago, the world was different. Two months ago, she was in her home on the northern edge of the woods. Her belly was huge then. Her woodsfolk neighbors would rub it for good luck every time they saw her. At first, Ashe hated the attention, but eventually, she learned to let it be.

Elfred, her husband, tended their small patch of land by day—their few crops were mostly potatoes, green onions, sour melons, and pears—always keeping a watchful eye on her. She enjoyed helping him with the picking, but her pregnancy prevented her from standing for too long. So Elfred set a chair outside their home for Ashe to rest and enjoy the cool Spring air.

The two of them had met when they were very young. Their parents were neighbors and close ones at that, which was common for woodsfolk who saw neighborliness as a sacred act. Ashe had been sweet on Elfred since the beginning—his uncommon pale-blonde hair always drawing her gaze—but the clueless boy never so much as paid her any mind. That was until she stole a kiss from him at a bonfire one Summer evening. That stolen kiss became hundreds more, and they eventually married and built a home for themselves.

Ashe had thought she was going to die when their daughter was born. The pain had been like nothing she had ever felt—its talons gripping into her for what seemed like forever. Finally, after much effort, their baby girl entered the world. She didn't cry at first, her big dark eyes peering around the room as if looking for something. The midwife picked the girl up and spanked her pink buttock, causing her to produce a hearty wail. They named her Sesha, after one of Elfred's aunts. The name meant 'bold and immediate' in the old tongue—it fit her like a glove.

But then the fires came. Ashe had awakened in the dead of night to the sound of distant booms as if a giant from the stories had been taking a stroll through Albadone. Their house rattled as the earth quaked beneath. Ashe stood from the cot she shared with Elfred and headed out of their room to look out the south-facing window: a strange white and orange glow filled the sky in the distance. As the tremors subsided somewhat, the booming sound grew, distant, at first, then much closer. Suddenly, the house went up in flames. She didn't see how it started—it was as if the fire had washed over the place like a wave.

She looked through the wall of flame that barred the doorway in horror—its ominous white and red glow was blinding in, what was moments ago, a dark room. Ashe bolted for Sesha's room, her eyes watching the flames crawl across the walls and floor to make their way to the baby's small crib—she and Elfred had spent an entire afternoon building it. The crib now looked like a pyre. Sesha lay unmoving among the flames that gnawed at her flesh like vermin. Without thought, Ashe reached into the fire and pulled out her baby, then ran outside through an opening that had formed in a collapsed wall.

She held onto Sesha tightly—the baby was still breathing, but Ashe dared not look at her in fear of what she might see. The house was lost to the flames. She called out for Elfred again and again—the name burned her lungs. Her calls became coughs, as dark smoke surrounded her. No answer ever came. In a panic, she ran into the woods. Sesha needed her. Elfred would find them.

Tears streaming down her face, Ashe didn't stop until she reached Peyta's house nearby. The old neighbor woman stood outside her home with her orphaned grandson Stetten. The young man was hardly sixteen, but he towered over his grandmother by at least two feet. Stetten was banging a shovel on the head of a long wooden post, setting it firmly into the dirt, as his grandmother supervised attentively—the woman held in her arms several other similar posts. As soon as Peyta laid her gray eyes on Ashe, she dropped the bundle onto the ground and led her inside, no questions asked.

"Keep setting the *Wards*," she instructed Stetten. "Leave enough room between them, but not too much."

Inside the cabin, Ashe recognized the familiar lingering scent of fresh herbs that had been there since the first time she visited many years earlier—their fragrance made her realize just how strongly the smell of smoke pervaded the forest. Peyta took Sesha from Ashe's trembling arms and set the poor girl on the cleared dining table. Ashe barely caught a glimpse of her baby, but what she saw made her sick to her stomach. Before she knew it, the world tipped over on its side and Ashe crumbled to the floor.

When she came to—perhaps the next morning, but Ashe couldn't be sure—she was on a cot, her arms and hands wrapped in clean white bandages. When had she burned herself? "Where's my baby?" she tried to ask, but the words came out in a wheeze. As if reading her mind, Peyta brought Sesha to her, the woman's leathery face contorted sourly. The poor child was wrapped from head to toe in white bandages.

"Her wounds are severe," the old woman said. "I'm no healer, so there's not a whole lot more I can do for her." She produced a purple runestone and set it on the bed next to Ashe. "I purchased this runestone of *Life* last year. I want you to have it. It won't heal her, but it should keep her alive and reduce her pain, at least until you can find someone that can heal her properly."

Ashe reached for the runestone with her bandaged hand. Prickles of heat shot up her fingers as she ran them across the stone's smooth surface. She opened her mouth and tried to thank the old woman, but all that came out was a whimper. She tried again after clearing her throat but, once more, she could produce nothing but the faintest airy sounds.

The old woman shook her head. "I'm sorry, dear. It seems you've breathed in too much hot smoke. It will take time for your voice to heal, if ever."

Ashe held onto Peyta's arm, gritting her teeth through the pain that stabbed at her hand, and did her best to mouth her husband's name. The old woman turned away and walked to a cauldron that hung over the fireplace to stir it—perhaps just to have something to do. "Dear..." she started. She didn't have to say more for Ashe to understand. "I wish I had good news for you—True One knows you need it. The fires have yet to die down. The woods are still ablaze with no sign of stopping any time soon. All that's keeping us protected are the *Wards* Stetten set outside. I truly doubt Elfred is alive. I'm so sorry."

Tears glistened on Ashe's cheeks. She could feel it in her heart that Elfred no longer lived, but the hope that he might have somehow survived had remained like a dying ember—now that hope had been put out. There was only her and Sesha now, and her daughter's life was hanging by a thread. Sesha whimpered, her cry sounding more like a coughing fit.

"She's hungry," Peyta said. Ashe looked down at her child, the cloth bandages covered her face, except for small openings that allowed for the baby's mouth and eyes to peek through. Her heart sank at the sight of what was underneath—her poor girl. Ashe released a breast from the gown the old woman had changed her into and lifted the child's gray mouth to her nipple. While the child's cries were placated, Ashe's grew into sobs.

In the time that Ashe remained with Peyta and Stetten, she tried to keep busy as best as she could—by cooking dinner, boiling water, and tidying up; there wasn't much else she could do with her arms the way they were. Then, ten days later, a heavy rain came and stifled the flames, clearing a path for Ashe to leave in the search of a healer for her child.

"Here, take this," the old woman said, placing an engraved dagger into Ashe's hand. "It was my late husband's. My grandson is here to keep me safe, so I have no need for it." Her voice lowered, almost to a whisper. "We don't know what has become of Albadone. In times of distress, neighbor may turn on neighbor, but if the True One places a helper in your path, don't hesitate to follow. I recommend you head for Pevine. They have some healers there."

The woman then gave Ashe a leather drinking sack full of water and a bundle filled with nuts and dried meats and fruit. "That should last you a couple of weeks if you portion it right," she explained. Ashe thanked Peyta with a hug. The old woman smiled, but the deep-set wrinkles at the sides of her eyes betrayed worry. Ashe left the cabin and walked into the thick gray woods.

The next five days on foot were rough. Sesha was wrapped firmly against her back. For the most part, the baby was quiet—the girl had always loved to observe the world around her with those large brown eyes; it seemed her burns hadn't changed that. Sometimes, however, she was too quiet. Ashe had to learn to read the baby's smallest motions: when she was hungry or needed relief from her wounds, she would kick her feet into Ashe's back. Ashe would stop, unwrap Sesha, and set her on the ground to assess what the baby needed.

If she wasn't hungry, that meant she was feeling the pain from her burns. Ashe would gently rub the purple runestone across the baby's small body. After a few moments,

Sesha would stop wiggling about as the pain faded away. In the first few days of travel, Ashe only had to use the runestone once a day. Then once a day became twice a day. And, by the fifth day, three times. It seemed as if Sesha was growing worse, and the effects of the runestone would eventually not be enough—not to mention there was always the possibility that the runestone could be spent; any time she used it could be the last.

With her back to a charred tree, Ashe allowed the baby to gently suckle from her breast. Sitting for so long made Ashe aware of the pain that coursed through her body. She tried to distract herself by looking at her surroundings, although there wasn't much to see through the thick grayness. The fires had burned the grass, exposing a layer of singed dirt and angular rocks. Among the rocks near where she sat, one stood out: a perfectly round stone. She picked it up, running her fingers across its smooth gray surface. The stone appeared reflective, a pale glow bouncing off of it. Something about that stone—perhaps its lack of hard edges among its sharp surroundings—made her slip it into her bag.

Once Sesha was satiated, she was returned to the wrap tied around Ashe's back. Soon after, they reached the point where the Chleo river bent southward. Pevine would be next, southwest from there. Ashe pulled the now empty leather drinking skin from her bag and bent over the river to refill it. Just before reaching into the water, she looked upstream: the rotting corpses of several deer lay in the water, crows picking bits of flesh off them. The deer's fur was singed and burned—most likely they had run for the water when the fires started. Who knew how many other animals had done the same? She would have to wait until she reached Pevine to have a drink.

Before standing, she caught a glimpse of her reflection in the murky water. Her face was gaunt, her cheekbones much more angular than she remembered them. She was a different woman now. Everything was different after the fires.

As she neared the town, she saw more and more people, all gathered about, camping in shabby tents that lined the road. Their faces were all marred by the same look of gray desperation. Unattended children sat on the ground, shoeless and hungry—some naked. A group of men and women were tossing corpses into a rotting pile—some had clearly perished from burns, while others must have died of hunger, Ashe reasoned. It was a bad sign. Ashe had hoped to find some respite in Pevine, but it seemed that desperation had overtaken the place. Soldiers stood out from the crowd in their clean red uniforms—the yellow sparrow on their chest marked them as being from Vizen. The Royals must have sent them to ensure that order was kept in Pevine, but, based on the way the townsfolk looked at them, it seemed some tension was simmering just underneath the surface.

Ashe followed the trail of refugees to the town. A tall wooden barricade encircled and blocked access into Pevine. A large crowd of blank-faced men, women, and children stood in front of it. The Vizen soldiers were stationed at the mouth of the barricade blocking all passage, their hands on their spears, expectantly. A fat man donned in a blue velvet doublet sat behind a table, holding a handkerchief over his nose to spare himself the scent of the unwashed masses.

A woodsfolk family—a man, woman, and two boys—at the front of the crowd appeared to be arguing with the man. Ashe only caught the tail end of it. "Either you show me your proof of residence, or you will not be allowed in," the fat man scoffed. "It is that simple."

The family's patriarch dropped two heavy fists onto the table. "We don't have any such proof," he yelled. "Why do I have to prove that I live someplace? You're not even from here! Who gives you the right to—" Before he could finish his argument, a soldier hit him on the side of the head with a gauntleted fist. The man fell limply to the ground as his wife screamed.

"Take him away," the fat man said to the woman, waving his hand as if swatting a gnat. "And make sure he does not return, lest I have him arrested."

The woman picked her husband up with the help of their two boys, quietly weeping as she did. The side of the unconscious man's face was already turning purple. The fat man shook his head at the pitiful sight, then stood to his feet—he was as short as he was round. "Excuse me," he called out, trying to get the crowd's attention. "Let me be as clear as a Sol Forne vintage, so that we may avoid any further incidents. Anyone that does not possess proof of residence in the town of Pevine, will not be allowed access. Am I understood?"

The crowd erupted into shouts of protest and rushed at the table with such urgency that the fat man had to back away with a start. Someone barked a command, and all the soldiers fixed their spears forward. The crowd immediately quieted down and backed away. Ashe felt a tinge of desperation hit her. Without proof of residence, there was no way she could enter Pevine. As she turned away from the crowd, she felt something tug at her sleeve. A young woodswoman, perhaps a few years younger than herself, stood behind her. The woman's blue eyes were fixed on Sesha.

"What's her name?" the woman asked in a friendly tone.

Sesha was an easy enough name to mouth, even without a voice.

"Come with me," the woman said, her eyes never leaving the baby.

Ashe should have felt apprehension, but something about this woman was calming to her. *If the True One places a helper in your path, don't hesitate to follow*, Peyta had told her.

"How old is your baby?" the woman asked.

"*Healer*," was all Ashe managed to get out in a hoarse whisper.

"No healers in Pevine," the woman said, finally turning her eyes to Ashe—they were not just blue, but also gray, with a splash of yellow near the center. "Those that survived the fires were taken to Lorne and Vizen to help there. I guess we're not as important." The seed of Ashe's desperation took root. "But we have some balms that may help and a change of bandages."

That was well and all, but how was Ashe supposed to enter the town? The young woman looked around as if to ensure no one was listening. She moved her head close to Ashe's ear. "I can get you in," she whispered, reading Ashe's mind.

Ashe tilted her head as if to ask, *and how do you intend on doing that?* Without adding more, the young woman took Ashe's arm and walked her to the table. The fat man looked up at them as if they were transparent. "Yes?" he asked, annoyed.

The young woman pulled out a wrinkled piece of paper from her hood and handed it to the man, who eyed it almost dismissively. "And who is this?" he asked, looking at Ashe, the handkerchief returning to cover his nose.

"My cousin Yeisha and her daughter." The young woman lied masterfully.

"Your cousin," the man repeated, glancing back and forth between the two of them, trying to notice some family resemblance. "I see." The man handed the young woman her paper and pointed towards the opening of the barricade. "Through there."

The young woman bowed in thanks and moved towards the town entrance. Ashe copied the woman's bow and then followed. A soldier led the two women through.

Ashe knew Pevine must have seen better days. She had never been in the town before—nor had she ever so much as seen a proper town in her entire life—but she could tell this wasn't what one was supposed to look like. On the northeastern side, several buildings lay in a pile of rubble and ashes. On the other, the street was littered with makeshift tents—some assembled out of what appeared to be curtains and bedsheets—full of families somberly eating meager meals together. Many had nothing at all. Two teenaged boys were carrying the body of a dead woman out of a building and loading it into the back of a mule cart. Soldiers patrolled the streets, their clean red uniforms forming a stark contrast with their gray, soot-covered surroundings. The smell of death filled every corner of the town. While there was plenty going on, a strange sober silence pervaded the scene, as if the inhabitants were afraid of making any sound.

"By the way, my name is Alanda," the young woman said as she led Ashe through the dreary streets. Surrounded by all that misery, Alanda's sweet round face was a well of fresh water after a long journey.

Ashe managed to mouth her own name—it was clear enough, the '*sh*' sound being one of the only ones she could still produce.

"You breathed in the smoke," Alanda concluded. "That happened to some folk here in town. Some of their voices have returned, while others... well, others still haven't. I hope yours returns to you soon. A child needs to hear their mother's voice."

Alanda stopped in front of a dilapidated building. A beaten old sign that must have hung over the door before the fires lay on the ground. It read: *The Rat's Nest*. What could have been an inviting tavern before was now as barricaded as the town entrance.

"This is *the Nest*, my family's tavern and home," Alanda explained.

At the door, Alanda knocked three times, taking an intentional pause between the second and third knock. After a few moments, the sound of rattling wood came from inside. The door opened, revealing an ominous darkness within. Alanda grabbed hold of Ashe's hand and led her inside. *If the True One places a helper in your path, don't hesitate to follow.*

XV.

The Rat's Nest

The tavern was aptly named. The main hall consisted of an old beaten wooden bar built into the right-side wall—the shelves behind it were soot-covered and barren; a door next to the shelves sat slightly ajar, revealing the flickering glow of candles within. The tables and chairs that would have filled the space had been turned into kindling, most of it piled against the left-side wall while the rest was burning in the large fireplace. The oppressive smell of smoke was pressed into the walls—no amount of cleaning could rid the tavern of it. But there was something else there too, underneath—the spiky scent of decay.

The woman that had unlocked the door hugged Alanda. She wore a dark scarf wrapped around her head that covered her face entirety except for her striking honey-colored eyes. Those eyes stopped on Ashe and Sesha, full of apprehension.

"This is Ashe," Alanda introduced. "She is a friend."

"Let's hope so," the woman replied. She sounded much younger than Ashe had assumed based on the slight limp the woman had when she moved. "I think he's still reciting his afternoon chants, but I'll go get him for you," the woman added and walked through the door behind the bar, closing it after her.

Alanda rubbed Ashe's shoulder, gently. "Don't mind her. She doesn't trust anyone as of late." Ashe nodded in a gesture of understanding. "Say," Alanda continued, "are you by any chance hungry?"

Ashe opened her sack and pulled out the empty leather drinking skin.

"Thirsty?" Ashe nodded. The young woman took the drinking skin from Ashe and smiled—the dimples that formed in her cheeks made her even more lovely. "Let me fetch some for you. There should be some already boiled." Alanda ducked behind the bar. On the floor sat a tall clay vase-like container. With a wooden ladle, Alanda filled the drinking skin with water, doing her best to not waste a drop.

"It has gotten harder and harder to find a reliable source of drinking water," Alanda explained. "Most of the nearby wells have dried up or were destroyed by the fires. That's why I was outside the town when we met: to search for neighboring wells or even any rumors of them. As it turns out, most people have been leaving for Vizen or taking the *Yellow Road* northward to test their luck in Perimat. Information is reaching Pevine late because of the blockade, and it's getting increasingly more dangerous to venture out each day."

Alanda left the ladle in the container and handed the full drinking sack back to Ashe. Ashe gulped greedily, drops of water running down the sides of her face. Sesha began to wiggle about and fuss in her wrap. Alanda smiled warmly and gently rubbed Sesha's bandaged cheek. "The poor child..." she said. "Set her on the bar. I can fetch some clean dressings for her. By the smell, I think she could use a change."

Alanda vanished through the door behind the bar. Ashe set her bag on the floor, unwrapped Sesha from her back, and placed the girl on the bar. Either she had grown used to Sesha's smell, or she stank badly herself—she flushed with embarrassment at the thought. From her cloth bag she produced the purple runestone. As she ran it gently across Sesha's body, the baby kicked the air and made gasping sounds—her way of crying.

"The power of folks' greed is a destructive force," a man's voice stated in a calm tone. Ashe looked up with a start as a short man donned in priestly white robes—well, they had been white before the soot had stained them—entered the main hall of the tavern through the door at the back of the bar. His round face was made rounder by the lack of hair on his head and face. The woman wrapped in the scarf followed him closely.

"If only we were blessed with the True One's foresight," he continued, "we would have stopped to appreciate what we had without wanting for more. But the True One didn't make folk to be content and appreciative. In our wickedness, we are compelled to strive for more, for something... greater than ourselves. Greed is in our lifeblood."

The man's expression was friendly enough, but Ashe was hesitant to lower her guard. Thankfully, Alanda entered the main hall with towels and strands of cloth in her arms—Ashe wasn't sure why, but she felt she could trust the young woman. "Her name is Ashe." Alanda gestured to the child, "And that's baby Sesha."

"Well, Ashe and Sesha," the man said, savoring their names—or, at least, seeing how they tasted on his tongue. "You're more than welcome to stay with us. We don't have much but, what we do have, we'll share."

"Father, we don't even know her," the woman with the wrapped face argued.

"But of course we do," the man answered. "We are all children of the True One. To know Him means to know all of His creation." The man returned his attention to Ashe. Taking a step towards her, he carried on solemnly, "My name is Yvan. I am High Priest of the True One's temple of Pevine. Well, I was until it was destroyed by the fires." A friendly smile remained on his mouth but didn't touch his eyes. "It appears you've already met my daughter Alanda. This is my youngest, Neverene." The woman bowed her wrapped head slightly in a reluctant greeting.

Alanda set her bundle of clean towels and cloth bandages onto the bar. "There's a basin in the back where you may wash up. I can change her for you; I've done it before." Ashe didn't enjoy the idea of leaving Sesha alone with a woman she had just met, but there was a warmth in Alanda's eyes that convinced her to agree. "Neverene," Alanda called, turning to her sister, "show Ashe to the back."

With a disgruntled sigh, Neverene led Ashe through the door behind the bar. The area must have been some sort of kitchen, judging by the dirty cookware and broken remains of plates and mugs littering the floor. Curing meats and aging cheeses hung from the ceiling, filling the kitchen with a sweet and earthy smell that barely covered the ever-present smell of smoke and soot. The space was rather dark—the sole window was boarded up, and the faint glow of two candles did a poor job of lighting the area. At the far end of the kitchen were two closed doors and, to their left, a staircase that led to the floor above.

"Here you are," Neverene said, pointing Ashe to a small wooden basin. A seemingly unused bar of herbal soap and a folded towel were set out for her as well. "Don't use too much soap," the woman added as she left the room. "That's all we have left."

Ashe dabbed the towel in the basin, and then lathered the soap against the wet area of the cloth, careful to use the resource sparingly. Meticulously, she began to clean her face and neck. The realization of how much she had truly needed a wash fully hit her as she saw how dark the water in the basin turned when she dipped the towel again. She must have looked just awful walking into town—that certainly explained the fancy-dressed man's expression upon seeing her, no—she cringed—*smelling* her.

"When you've finished washing, please, come with me." She hadn't heard the high priest enter the room. Something about the man's smile made her nervous—perhaps it was the faint lighting of the candles that was adding a sinister glow to his face. She nodded in response, and the man disappeared through a door in the far corner of the kitchen.

Once she had cleaned her legs and feet and patted herself dry, Ashe entered the room where Yvan had gone. The small office was filled almost entirely by a table, three chairs, and a large steel safe. Yvan motioned for Ashe to take a seat. Once she did, he closed the door and sat across from her, folding his hands. His smile turned into a worried scowl.

"My daughter tells me something is the matter with your voice, so I'll try to ask questions that require a 'yes' or 'no' as answers. You see, around them, I must maintain the illusion of control. I am a pious man, have been my entire life, but recent circumstances have made me rethink the way I approach people. I must do all I can to ensure my daughters' safety. You can understand that?"

Ashe swallowed a thick lump in her throat. A sudden fear for Sesha made her heartbeat quicken. She answered Yvan with a nod. Tension left the man's face, but only partially.

"Now, let's get to the meat of it," he continued. "Do you mean me, or my daughters any harm?"

Ashe shook her head.

"Then you won't mind if I hold onto this?" Yvan pulled Peyta's engraved dagger from his robe. Ashe's heart sank, but all she could do was shake her head. Yvan placed the dagger back in his robe. "That's good to hear." He must have noticed Ashe's sullen expression because he quickly added, "If you fear for your child's life, you can rest assured that she will be kept safe. Even if you harmed us, we would not act against her. There are some teachings of the True One that must always be upheld, especially in times such as these."

Ashe feigned a smile and nodded, as if to thank him—in truth, the man's words hadn't put her at ease one bit. "I also saw that you had this with you." Yvan placed the purple runestone on the table. "I apologize once again for rummaging through your belongings, but every precaution must be taken when dealing with strangers in these times. This runestone of *Life*, did an enchantress give it to you?"

Ashe shook her head.

"A neighbor, then?" When Ashe nodded, the man smiled, this time with a bit more warmth. "The True One said to always trust in the kindness of neighbors. That's why we woodsfolk form such tightly knit communities. This runestone, it won't heal your child, you know this?"

Ashe lowered her eyes. Yvan took that for assent.

"Did you come to Pevine for your child? To search for a healer, yes?"

Ashe studied the man—something had changed in both his face and demeanor. Was that compassion she saw bubbling to the surface? She nodded.

"I'm sorry to say, there are no healers in Pevine," he replied, "or chemists," he added almost as an afterthought, rubbing his hands together. "Most of them have been hauled off to the bigger cities as if the folk here aren't made of the same meat and lifeblood." Yvan handed Ashe the purple runestone. He then produced the smooth round stone Ashe had found in the woods, setting it onto the table with as much reverence as he had the runestone.

"And this," Yvan continued, "where did you come upon this?

Ashe shrugged, unsure of why the man would care.

"Do you know what this is?" Ashe shook her head. Yvan paused briefly as if to puzzle something out. "This is a runestone of *Guidance*. It's almost fully spent, but there's no mistaking that's what it is. Did someone give this to you also?"

Ashe shook her head.

"With this, you'll be able to find anything you conjure in your mind." Yvan slid the smooth stone across the table, towards Ashe. She took the runestone in her hands, only then seeing the three concentric circles etched on its surface. "Use that stone wisely," Yvan warned. "I'm not sure it has more than one use left before it's fully spent."

The gray stone clinked against the purple runestone in Ashe's pocket.

"As I'm now convinced you mean us no harm, you may stay with us at least a few days. We have some food left and room enough for you and your child." He sighed. "It will be dark soon, and Pevine has become a dangerous place when darkness falls." Admitting that seemed to pain him. "It's good to see my daughter Alanda smile again." He was looking at Ashe but not really seeing her. "She had a child too, before the fires. I've never seen anyone built for being a mother as she. Why the True One decided to take her child away in such a manner is a question to which I'm not sure I'll ever find an answer."

Yvan dismissed her, but he remained seated in the office. Ashe followed the kitchen back to the main hall of the tavern. Alanda was walking slowly while patting Sesha gently on the back. "She's asleep," Alanda whispered. Ashe smiled. Yvan was right—it was as if the young woman was made for this.

Neverene was stirring something over the fireplace. There wasn't much of a smell to it, so it couldn't have been anything too involved. "It's all we got," the woman spat in an annoyed tone when Ashe went to peek. Ashe was hungrier than she had realized, so even 'all we got' sounded delightful to her. "Don't go getting fussy about it. Either you eat or you don't."

In the pot, several browning potatoes were bobbing sadly in the boiling water. "I used to cook great roasts every night when *the Rat's Nest* was open," the woman reminisced. "Amazing roasts, I tell you! With all sorts of carrots: red, purple, and white." Noticing that Ashe's eyes were on her, Neverene tugged at her scarf, pulling it closer to cover her eyes. "I'd prefer if you did not stare."

Ashe nodded an apology and walked away. She sat on the floor, her back to a wall. A peaceful air descended upon the place—there was some sense of normalcy that had finally been restored to her from before the fires. As the pot quietly bubbled and Alanda gently shushed the baby, Ashe found herself falling into a deep, dark, and dreamless sleep.

A banging sound jolted her awake. Alanda stood at the back of the hall, Sesha wrapped tightly in her arms. Neverene and Yvan both stood near the door, as someone on the other side knocked with a heavy fist.

"How many of you are there?" Yvan asked.

"It's just... two of us," the man on the other side called out.

"Father, he's lying," Neverene protested. "I heard at least four voices."

The man outside responded by kicking at the door and yelling, "Let us in, old man!"

Ashe stood and walked to Alanda and Sesha—the baby had awakened; she was kicking her legs about, fussing. "They do this at times," Alanda explained, worry marring her lovely face. "We've let folk in before, and they stole all our gold, silverware, and drink..." Her voice lowered to a whisper. "They did terrible things to us... To Neverene..."

The banging at the door and the yelling outside grew exponentially—it seemed as if several men had joined in. Yvan reached into his hood and pulled out Peyta's dagger, holding it in a quivering hand. By the look of him, the man had most likely never wielded a weapon before.

"Go to the back," Yvan called to no one in particular. Alanda quickly took Sesha to the kitchen, followed by a reluctant Neverene. "Go!" Yvan yelled at Ashe, who was still standing in the hall.

Leaving the man there, alone, didn't feel right to Ashe; but her baby always came first. She was headed for the kitchen door when a sudden crash sounded in the hall.

Ashe ducked behind the bar as three men squeezed into the tavern, circling Yvan like a pack of hungry wildcats. Outside, several other men stood and watched with blank expressions. Yvan pointed the knife at the townsman closest to him—a youth of about sixteen with mud-caked hair and a ferocious look in his eye. The young man laughed and slapped the dagger out of Yvan's hand with ease.

"Were you planning on attacking us, old man?" the young intruder mocked. He smacked Yvan across the face, sending the old priest to the floor. "I thought your True One taught you to be kind to your neighbors. Keeping us out isn't very neighborly, now, is it?"

"I'll give you whatever you want," Yvan pleaded, holding his bruised cheek. "Just please, let us be."

"And what if what I want is this entire tavern? Will you give me that? What about your life? Can I have that too?" The youth spoke with a bloodthirsty grin. "My mother says your 'True One' is what caused all this. If that's true, then you woodsfolk all deserve some sort of punishment."

"The True One—" Yvan's words were interrupted by a fist to the face. The townsman kneeled and placed his hands around the old priest's neck. The other men laughed as Yvan coughed and choked.

"Watch him turn into a blueberry," one of them mocked.

A sudden flash of panic—or perhaps stupidity—made Ashe jump over the bar. She snatched the dagger sitting on the floor and began stabbing the young man in the back again and again. There was a sort of frantic joy to it—a rightness. The startling relief she felt was like the setting of a joint she hadn't known was dislocated. The crowd outside scattered, as the other men in the tavern stood there staring as their friend fell to the ground screaming in a pool of his own blood—at least, Ashe had assumed they were friends; she wasn't so convinced anymore. Ashe stood to her feet, pointing the blade at the nearest man, her eyes wide and feral. Now it was their turn to be afraid. The man bolted out of the tavern, followed by the rest of the townsmen. They stood outside watching her with shocked expressions until Ashe shut the door in their faces.

Yvan was in the midst of a coughing fit, struggling to catch his breath. Purple veins seemed to want to burst at his temples. Neverene ran out from the kitchen door to kneel over him. "Father," she yelled. "Are you all right?" Yvan nodded between coughs. Neverene's eyes then turned to the young man bleeding on the floor and finally to the bloody blade in Ashe's hand. "You did that?" she asked calmly as if inquiring about what was for dinner. Ashe nodded. She couldn't be entirely sure, but Ashe thought she noticed a spark of glee flash in the woman's eyes. "We'll have to patch him up, I guess. The True One would want us to, right father?"

Yvan's coughing had dissipated, but his breath was still ragged and heavy. "The True One is a merciful god." From his tone, Ashe could sense that the man wished it weren't so in this case. Neverene nodded. She helped her father to his feet and then headed for the kitchen with almost exaggerated leisure.

Yvan's eyes were fixed on the dagger in Ashe's hand—she had, for a moment, forgotten it was still there. She went to hand it back to him, but the priest held his hand up to stop her. "Perhaps it is best if you hold onto it," he said.

Neverene emerged into the main hall, carrying a pile of clean towels. "I can't believe we're wasting our clean linens on this townsman," she muttered, just loudly enough to be heard.

Ashe entered the kitchen and washed the bloody knife in the basin. The bandages that covered her arms were also soaked in the young man's blood. Carefully, she unwrapped them from her arms—they were sticky and hard to remove. She didn't like looking at the burns that covered her arms and rendered them unrecognizable. The wounds needed cleaning. Pus and other stinking fluids had built up; the scent of putrefaction was a sharp warning—she could only imagine the pain her baby must be feeling.

She suddenly noticed Alanda standing next to her, eyeing her wounds warily. Where was Sesha?

"I put the baby to bed," Alanda said as if reading Ashe's mind. "She's very fussy. I think she's in pain." Alanda dumped out the basin of murky water and filled it with some that had been freshly boiled. With a sponge, she helped Ashe clean her arms. The pain was hot fire against her tortured flesh. Was this the same pain that Sesha felt every waking moment?

When her wounds were sufficiently cleaned, Alanda wrapped them in clean bandages. Ashe nodded in thanks and then coughed out her daughter's name.

"Follow me," Alanda replied, leading her upstairs.

The upstairs hallway was even darker than the kitchen as it had neither windows nor candles to brighten it. Alanda guided Ashe through the blackness into a bedroom illuminated by faint candlelight. The windows had been boarded up, like all the others in the tavern. Two small cots and a wardrobe populated the small place. Sesha lay atop one of the cots, wiggling and crying in the pitiful way she could manage.

Ashe sat next to her baby and produced the purple runestone from her pocket. Alanda watched attentively as Ashe used the runestone to soothe her child. Eventually, the baby quieted and fell asleep. Ashe turned to look at Alanda—the woman's eyes were filled with tears that glittered in the candlelight. When Alanda noticed she was being observed, she turned abruptly to the door.

"We'll be serving dinner soon," she said as she left the room.

XVI.

A Dark Escape

Dinner tasted as bland as it had looked: boiled potatoes in broth. A single bone contributed the faint memory of beef—no doubt it had seen several uses before this. Ashe didn't mind a bit. She finished her bowl voraciously then held it out for seconds.

"I know it's awful," Neverene said sardonically. "You don't have to give me false compliments."

"I think she's simply hungry," Alanda said, cracking a slight smile while looking at Ashe. There was a sadness that could be easily missed behind the woman's eyes. Ashe knew that pain well. That she was able to smile at all was nothing short of a miracle.

Neverene refilled Ashe's bowl with a second helping of potatoes, which Ashe devoured just as quickly—she had sustained herself on dried meats and fruits for long enough that potatoes felt like a delicacy. Although Neverene felt the dish wasn't something to be proud of, she seemed pleased by Ashe's enjoyment of both helpings.

They shared the dinner in the small office. Yvan hadn't joined, as he felt unwell after the assault he had endured. The priest would take his dinner in his bedroom when he was up for it. Ashe had left Sesha asleep on the cot upstairs after passing the purple runestone over her small body. It had been the third time she had done so that day—either the effects of the runestone were diminishing, or Sesha's condition was growing worse; both options were doom. The baby needed a healer, and if there weren't any to be found in Pevine, Ashe would have to leave soon in search of one.

Before dinner, Neverene had cleaned the young intruder's stab wounds and wrapped him in clean bandages, muttering curses under her breath the entire time. Blood had reddened the bandages almost immediately—without a healer on hand, those wounds would most likely keep bleeding. Nevertheless, Neverene had laid the man on the floor of the main hall and placed a pillow under his head and a blanket over his shivering body. He wouldn't survive the night.

After dinner, Neverene sat next to the townsman, stating that she would stay with him until the end—it was the neighborly thing to do. Ashe tried to feel bad for hurting the young man, but she just couldn't—Alanda insisted that she had saved them all. Ashe couldn't bring herself to consider what might have happened had she not acted.

Sesha was still asleep when Ashe entered the dimly lit room. The candle at the window fluttered as it struggled to stay alive. Ashe lay next to her baby, not bothering to undress—she had been on the move for so long that being in one place felt suddenly unfamiliar. Alanda entered the room soon after, undressed to her smallclothes, and took over the other cot. They remained silent as the candle flickered out, leaving them in total darkness. Ashe could hear Alanda's breathing from the other side of the room. She wished she could say something to the woman, ask her about her child.

Ashe heard Neverene's soft footsteps climbing the staircase and heading into the room—the young man must have passed. Neverene removed the scarf from her head—Ashe could only make out the silhouette of the woman's hair cascading down her back, long and luscious—and lay on the cot next to her sister.

Ashe couldn't sleep. Maybe she had gotten too used to sleeping under burnt trees and bushes, she thought. But she hadn't slept then either—constantly worrying that she might miss her daughter's cries of pain. It could be the life she had ended that kept her awake. But if she hadn't done so, it would have been at the cost of someone else's, perhaps even Sesha's. As she lay there allowing the darkness to swallow her, she listened to the ragged rising and falling of her baby's chest. Dark thoughts began to haunt her. Where would she go once she left Pevine? They told her all the healers had been taken to the nearby cities, but even Vizen was several days away on foot. Would Sesha be able to make it that long? She would have to.

She kissed Sesha tenderly on her bandaged head and closed her eyes, hoping that she might get at least some rest before leaving at dawn. And sleep did come, enveloping her in its warm and dark embrace—but not for long. Ashe felt a tug at her sleeve. Her eyes shot wide open. In the darkness, she could make out Neverene standing over her, the woman's head once again wrapped in the scarf, and Alanda holding the baby near the door. Both women were fully dressed and booted.

"You must get up," Neverene said in a quivering voice. "They're coming!"

Ashe choked on the questions trapped in her throat. She quickly stood and looked at Alanda. "Some townsfolk are downstairs, breaking through the door," Alanda explained—the woman always seemed to sense exactly what Ashe needed to know. "We must hurry!"

Alanda returned the baby to Ashe and left the room followed by her sister. An orange glow seeped in through the boards at the window. Ashe followed the sisters downstairs, into the kitchen. The sound of smashing wood and the voices of a crowd of angry townsfolk erupted in the main hall of the tavern. Yvan held the door next to the office open. It led to a brightly lit alleyway behind the tavern—why was it so bright?

"I hoped and wished it would not come to this," Yvan said, rubbing his bruised neck nervously. "The poor souls have lost everything, including their way. In their loss, they see fit to—"

"This is no time for a sermon, father!" Neverene interrupted brusquely as she exited the kitchen.

Alanda grabbed Ashe's shoulder, her touch somehow always light, and nodded in the direction of the door. Holding onto Sesha tightly, Ashe hurried into the alleyway, Alanda and Yvan right behind. Neverene took the lead despite her limp, guiding them through the tight path. Screams filled the air—some angry and vile, others scared and suffering. The yellow-orange glow of fire illuminated the dark sky eerily, the gray haze that pervaded everything as of late now intertwined with dark smoke.

When the alleyway opened into the main street, the Pevine they saw was a much different one than that of the prior day. Several buildings were ablaze. Vizen soldiers chased small groups of folk, their spears drawn. A crying woman knelt beside a man who had been stabbed through the shoulder, his ragged breath making his chest quiver.

"True One!" Yvan exclaimed. "What has befallen Pevine?"

"Quiet, father!" Neverene shushed. "From here on out, we must remain calm and quiet. We have no other option but to leave Pevine, tonight."

"But we didn't bring any supplies with us," Yvan lamented. At the mention of supplies, Ashe realized she had left her bag in the building. In a panic she patted herself down: the dagger was there, as was the runestone of *Guidance* in her pocket, but she had left the purple runestone behind. She looked at the bandaged baby in her arms with regret and fear.

"Ashe, what is it?" Alanda asked. Ashe met Alanda's eyes, and somehow the woman understood what that panicked expression meant. "We can't go back. Let's focus on leaving Pevine first." Ashe nodded, but she couldn't help feeling the dreadful hand of panic squeeze the air out of her chest.

The screams that surrounded them grew louder, as a crowd of men and women swept past them in a single direction. "We must go," Neverene said, guiding them to join the crowd. As Neverene entered the stream of folk that was rushing by, she was immediately carried away by it, vanishing from sight.

The other four remained in the alleyway, watching as the sea of folk swelled into an ocean. Then, abruptly, the flow of the crowd ended. A row of soldiers marched behind— their spears herding the citizens of Pevine away from the barricade's only exit. After that row of soldiers, there was another. One of the men glanced in their direction and broke formation.

"You there!" he called out, his spear drawn and pointed at them threateningly. "All Pevine folk have been ordered to return to their homes." His voice was surprisingly calm, dispassionate even. "If you do not comply, you will be arrested. If you resist, the punishment is death."

Almost as an answer, a hatchet was buried into the back of the soldier's neck. The soldier lost his grip on the spear, letting it tumble to the ground as he fell to his knees. A woman with a crazed expression stood behind him, laughing as if she had just heard the funniest joke. She pulled the hatchet from the soldier's bleeding neck with remarkable ease and struck the man once more. The soldier fell to the ground limply, his head blooming red. Three nearby soldiers ran to the scene and skewered the woman with their spears as if she were a piece of feast day meat. Several other soldiers and folk joined the fray, each group attacking the other in a gruesome display.

Alanda took hold of Ashe's arm in one hand and Yvan's in the other—the high priest's face had drained of all blood—and guided them out of the alleyway and around the massacre that was materializing before them. As they pressed on through town, guided now by Alanda, the chaos grew worse: not one building in sight had been spared by the flames; the streets were lined with dead folk and soldiers—the bodies of the folk outnumbering the soldiers' at least five to one. But Alanda did not stop nor slow down: she led them steadily towards the front of the barricade. Most soldiers they encountered simply ran past them, headed deeper into town towards the fires and the rioting.

When they reached the entrance, the area was strangely calm—about four soldiers stood near the opening of the barricade; Ashe could see there were many more on the other side, however. When the soldiers saw them, they raised their spears to bar their way.

"Halt!" one of them yelled. "Return to your homes or you will be arrested."

"Our home has burned to the ground," Alanda yelled in response, her voice as calm as she could make it. "We have no place to return to. Please let us through. We have a baby with us that urgently needs a healer."

A murmur traveled between the soldiers. One slowly lowered his spear, and the others followed suit. "Which one is the baby's mother?" the same soldier asked.

Alanda let go of her father's arm and pushed Ashe gently in front of them. "This is her."

"Then she may take her child out of the town," the soldier replied. "The rest of you must stay here. If you have no home to return to, you may remain close by. We will protect you from the rioters."

Alanda turned to Ashe with a smile. "Hear that? Go!"

Ashe shook her head, scowling.

"Yes," Alanda replied to Ashe's protest. She was still wearing that beautiful, dimpled smile. She gently touched Sesha's head. "You are both very blessed to have each other. Protect her at all costs. I will keep you both in my heart."

"As will I," Yvan added in a frazzled voice. "We may have nothing material left to our names, but we still have our faith."

Ashe looked at Alanda, as tears forced their way out. Good folk were so few and far between. She may have only met Alanda the day before, but there was something special about the young woman; something she wasn't quite ready to let go of yet. Ashe pulled out her dagger and handed it to Alanda. The young woman opened her mouth to protest, but then she simply accepted it and placed it in her skirt.

"We have family in Rondhill," Alanda said. "When we find Neverene and are allowed to leave Pevine, we will most likely head there. When Sesha is healed, you should join us there. You will both always have a place with us. Now go, before they change their minds."

Ashe threw herself into Alanda's arms, hugging her fiercely. Alanda pressed her warm forehead onto Ashe's—it could have been her imagination, but Ashe could have sworn that she felt the True One tying their fates together. Reluctantly, she let go of Alanda and headed for the opening in the barricade. The soldiers parted to let her through.

"Make way!" The line of soldiers outside the town broke formation for her. Several of the refugees encamped outside stood watching the fires devour the town—no doubt many felt relief for not having been let in. For a few moments, Ashe stood there cradling Sesha and looking past the soldiers into the opening in the barricade—at Alanda. The woman's eyes were looking right back. Yvan appeared to be speaking to a soldier, possibly about Neverene. Then Alanda diverted her eyes and walked away until she was out of sight behind the barricade.

Ashe carried Sesha away past rows and rows of tents, most of their owners standing outside with their worried eyes set on the blazing town. Beyond the outcropping of tents, Sesha began to complain, kicking and crying softly. Ashe sat on the singed ground just off the road and unbuttoned her blouse. She placed the baby's mouth to her nipple and watched as she suckled. Soon, the poor girl would start to feel pain again. The thought made Ashe sick with grief. Without the purple runestone, Sesha was as good as dead. No! She couldn't go down that dark road; not yet.

A mule cart trotted up the beaten road, headed for Pevine. At the sight of the fires ahead, the mule halted in front of Ashe and shook its head, refusing to move forward. The driver jumped off the cart and looked out at the town. "What happened?" the driver asked a squat man that sat on the side of the road near a small tent. Inside the tent, a woman held onto a young girl, stroking her light hair lovingly.

"The townsfolk started a riot," the man explained. "The town is on fire, and many are likely dead if the screams we heard are any indication." The man seemed only then to notice the mule and the cart. "Are you coming from Vizen? How are things there?"

"Not too good," the driver replied. "King Petar had the bloody gates closed. Couldn't even cross the bridge to get close to the city. The ports are closed too. They say he shut everything up after taking in all the healers and chemists from every neighboring town and village. Lots of tension there too. People don't very much enjoy being locked into a place."

"You tell that to them," the man replied, pointing at the soldiers guarding the front of the barricade.

"No point in staying here, then," the driver said, mostly to himself. "Perhaps I'll try my luck north, in Perimat." The driver climbed back onto the cart and turned it around, with some resistance from the frightened mule.

Ashe looked at her child. If all the healers had been hauled to Vizen, where was she supposed to take Sesha? She could ask the driver for a ride, but, even by cart, a trip to Perimat could take several weeks—Sesha would never survive that long. She closed her blouse and rose in a panic. Ashe walked over to the squat man, pointing at her bandaged baby. The man grimaced, unable to understand what she was trying to communicate.

"Now, shoo, you," he said, swatting. "We don't have any food to spare."

Ashe shook her head, doubling down on pointing at her child and then at the mule cart already several feet away—even she was not entirely sure what she was trying to tell the confused man. Her communication was made more difficult as tears of frustration began to fall from her eyes.

"Please leave, or I'll remove you," the man said, chest out, in a halfhearted display of toughness.

"Calm down, dear," the woman inside the tent said—her voice an audible eye roll. "She's obviously concerned for her child." The woman crawled out of the tent and walked to Ashe. "Say," the woman continued, getting a closer look at Ashe. "Aren't you Elfred's wife?"

At the sound of her dead husband's name, Ashe's heart leaped. She nodded, forcing a smile through her tears.

"I remember you from the wedding," the woman said. "My name is Ezie. Elfred is my old neighbor's cousin. We lived near the Chleo, so every Summer Elfred used to come visit to take baths. How is he doing?" Ashe's smile vanished much faster than she had intended. The woman seemed to understand. "I'm sorry," she said. She attempted to change the subject. "You can't speak?"

Ashe shook her head while wiping the tears from her eyes.

"And you need a healer?"

Ashe nodded.

"Well, as you heard, there are none to be found anywhere. But I do know of someone that may be able to help you. Mother Adriel. She's an enchantress. She was Mother Olla's apprentice before the old woman passed."

Ashe had heard of Mother Olla—most folk had. She was supposed to have been the best enchantress that ever was. Surely her apprentice, this Mother Adriel, must have learned something useful from her.

"I'm not certain where she is exactly, but I heard she can be found at the Womb of the World these days. After tonight, I think we will be heading there soon as well. I'm more than certain she'll be willing to help you in any way she can."

Hope blossomed in Ashe's heart. She hugged the woman tightly.

"No need for thanks," Ezie said. "It's the neighborly thing to do." Her eyes shot daggers at her husband as she said it.

XVII.

To Sacrifice

E zie and her husband, Blatt, shared a small portion of dried goat jerky with her and one leather skin of water. It was all they could spare, and even then, Blatt did so begrudgingly.

"If we stop treating our neighbors as the True One has taught us, then we are no different than beasts," Ezie said pointedly.

Ashe waved goodbye and set off towards the Womb of the World. She didn't need directions: everyone in Albadone knew where the great mountain stood. It was visible even from the north where her home had been. Heading south into the darkness of early dawn, Ashe did her best to hold Sesha with gentle hands—the baby had been asleep ever since Ashe had nursed her. The moon and stars were hidden behind the thick omnipresent fog. The sole indication that time was passing was a slight change in the flat greyness of the sky to a pale bluish hue. As the sun rose, it painted the dead trees that surrounded her with purple and orange. Somehow, the fog made the sunrise more beautiful, diffusing the sunlight while sharp beams passed through bony branches as if cutting through the air.

From where she was, she should have been able to see the black mountain looming ahead, but the haze was so impenetrable that she could see only a few feet in front of her. This was both a detriment and a blessing, as it concealed her and Sesha from any person—or thing—that may want to do them harm. Having seen what had occurred in Pevine, the fear of being robbed, attacked, or worse, nipped at her back. But her concern for Sesha stood at the forefront of her mind. She hastened her step and carried on, through the fog, past unchanging terrain, towards a place she couldn't see—if it weren't for the sunrise guiding her sense of direction, she would have been entirely lost.

The hours began to bleed together. There was a kind of peace in being so alone, surrounded by an apparent nothingness but with a clear goal driving her onward. Since the fires, the songbirds had flown elsewhere, rendering the foggy landscape silent and still. Ashe's feet began to hurt, but she ignored their protests. There were times when her mind would drift, and she would have to remind herself where she was headed. How many hours had it been? Three, four, five? More?

By the time she reached the river, the sun was high in the midmorning sky. The river Ellot split from the Chleo and ran westward, towards the ocean. Ashe knew from the sight of it that she was nearing her destination. She hoped that once she reached the mountain, the enchantress would be easy to find. Sesha fussed and kicked her legs about, grunting and coughing angrily. There was nothing Ashe could do to soothe the child. Ashe held Sesha close to her breast and shushed her gently, with little effect. Without the purple runestone, the baby would soon succumb to her pain.

The deepest part of the river reached her thighs. The water was cold and soothing to her sore feet. The river was a few feet wide with a slow current, so Ashe reached the other bank easily. The terrain changed abruptly under her feet, becoming hard and rocky—she had arrived at the foot of the Womb. The fog cleared somewhat as she neared the mountain. As its sharp pointed edges came into view, towering over her like dark claws, the path she was on rose, growing even steeper. Ashe wished she could have called out for the enchantress. Instead, she scanned the sharp landscape for any sign that someone had been in the area. The climb was tricky, especially while holding a fussy baby. Most of the rocks that paved the path were sturdy, but their jagged edges demanded that she keep a watchful eye on her footing.

Ashe spotted a broken wooden wagon wheel lying on the side of the path. It was unweathered, so there must have been someone nearby recently. About half an hour later Ashe saw four tents planted inside a large opening in the side of the mountain. A townswoman was preparing food in a pot over a fire while another skinned a rabbit, as a child watched her attentively. The rest of the group—three men, a woman, and three other children, all townsfolk—were scattered about the small campsite napping, lounging, or playing. Two mules tied to a parked cart were lazily nibbling a bale of hay.

The first to see Ashe was a dark-haired little girl who pointed and called out for her parents. The entire campsite's eyes were suddenly on her. Ashe froze, waiting for them to say or do something. One of the townsmen stood and approached her, calmly. His graying hair had small remaining streaks of red from his younger years. "Hello," he greeted her curtly. He had clearly assessed that she was not a threat. "Is there anything we can do for you?" His tone was friendly enough, but there was a hint of weariness in it, as if he wished she'd simply move along.

Ashe licked her dry lips. The eyes of everyone in the campsite bored through her. She cleared her throat, hoping in vain that her voice would return. It didn't. She lifted Sesha towards the man. At the sight of the bandaged baby, his expression became one of concern.

A middle-aged townswoman, her long gray hair wrapped around her neck in a braid, ran up to join them. "What happened to the child?" she asked.

Ashe shook her head while holding her throat.

"You can't speak?" the man asked. Ashe nodded. She raised the child once more with urgency, trying desperately to impress upon them the importance of the matter. "We don't have medicine or a chemist with us," the man explained.

"Perhaps Mother Adriel could help," the woman suggested. Ashe nodded vigorously, stepping in closer to them.

It seemed as if they both understood her meaning. "You seek Mother Adriel," the woman confirmed. Ashe nodded once more, her impatience growing.

"I can take you to her," the man offered. "Well, she told us not to disturb her, so I can only take you close to where she is staying. Don't expect me to stick around for introductions."

Ashe nodded her thanks. At last, she felt as if she was making progress. The townsman picked up a canteen from where he had been lounging. With a nod, he led Ashe up the mountain. The eyes of the men, women, and children at the campsite remained on her until she was out of sight.

"Mother Adriel has been good to us," the man said, as he guided her up the path. "She knew something evil was going to happen in the forest, so she retreated to the Womb of the World. I was hired to transport her things from her old cabin to a cave in the mountain, mostly junk and quite a few large books. When I asked why she was leaving the forest, she warned me that a curse would befall Albadone, and to leave immediately if we wished to stay safe."

The man took a pull from his canteen. "So that's just what I did. And thank the gods I uprooted my family and came here! I warned some friends as well, and a few followed suit. It wasn't easy to convince my wife at first... She thought I had lost my mind. But I knew we would be safe if we stayed near Mother Adriel. We don't see the enchantress much, though. She prefers to stay alone. We gift her rabbits and anything else we catch to thank her for the warning."

His voice took on a darker tone. "Things must be pretty rough down there." It wasn't a question, and he didn't look to Ashe for a response. "After the fires, we could hear the screams and the cries for days, even from up here. It was a nightmare."

He didn't know the half of it. Ashe felt heat creep up her neck and a stab of anger. This enchantress had known the fires would occur and had done nothing about it but warn some townsfolk and leave. Woodsfolk were taught to respect enchantresses as if they were elders—how could she have allowed so many of her own people to die like that?

"It's not much farther," the townsman called after a bout of silence. The winding path turned and widened into a small rocky canyon. Several small caves dotted the side of the mountain like a honeycomb. "We're here," the man announced. "Mother Adriel lives over there." He pointed to a cave at the other end of the valley. A campfire burned at its threshold. "I must turn back now. I hope you'll find the help you seek." Ashe nodded, and the townsman turned to head down the path. From what she had been told about townsfolk, she had never expected to meet one so... *neighborly.*

As she approached the cave, Ashe felt sick to her stomach from the tension. Sesha was wiggling about restlessly. There was no time to hesitate. The smell of stewing meat emanated from the pot that sat over the fire and made her stomach twist in knots—True One, she was starving. A few candles were scattered about to illuminate the tight space. A humble cot lay on one side of the cave. A chest, some shelves of large dusty books, and a dresser whose refined beauty stood out like a gold piece in a chamber pot were on the other side.

"You're just in time for lunch." Ashe turned with a start, to find a young woman standing behind her. A yellow runestone at the woman's neck flashed in the daylight. Her brown hair was wildly scattered about, pointing in every direction, as if it hadn't seen a brush in months. While she was, indeed, quite young, the woman had a wisdom in her eyes, as if she carried within her truths from a distant time. She held a basket full of *poxcheek* mushrooms.

Ashe held Sesha out to the enchantress who, strangely enough, seemed to instantly understand. "Here," the enchantress said, handing Ashe the basket. "Put these in the pot, and make sure to stir often. I'll tend to the child." Ashe did as she was told, although she wasn't sure what *poxcheeks* would add to any stew with their overbearing woody flavor.

She poured the mushrooms into the bubbling stew and stirred it with a wooden spoon that had sat on the stones surrounding the fire. Her eyes, however, were intent on the enchantress and Sesha. The young woman laid the fussing baby on the black-stone floor and produced a purple runestone from a small container filled with other colorful stones. She began gently rubbing it across Sesha's body as Ashe had done many times before.

"You are aware this won't heal her." The enchantress stated it as a matter of fact. "I'm no healer, and this is the most I can do on such short notice. There is something else I could do for her, but it would take some time: an ancient ritual of strength that goes beyond simple enchanting." The enchantress picked Sesha up and placed her on the cot. The baby seemed soothed by the runestone. How long would that last? Mother Adriel selected two bowls from a shelf and handed one to Ashe. "Serve yourself."

Ashe didn't have to be asked twice. She scooped the stew into the bowl with the wooden spoon and began to drink it. It was warm and hearty, with bits of shredded rabbit meat, turnips, potatoes, and yellow carrots—where had the woman even found yellow carrots? The *poxcheeks* weren't her favorite, but she had to admit something about their silky texture was alluring. When she finished the stew, she realized Mother Adriel had been watching her with an amused expression.

"It's been a long while since I've had the opportunity to cook for anyone," the enchantress said. "I prefer to be left alone, but one must admit there is a joy to be had in watching a neighbor enjoy a meal you've prepared." Ashe smiled politely. In truth, she felt uncomfortable near the woman—she had spent so long wishing to be understood by those around her, and now Mother Adriel seemed to know entirely too much.

Mother Adriel smiled. "Let's get to it—you're here because of your daughter, not for my cooking. She was burned in the great fire, as were you, it appears. I can help her: remove her burns and ensure that she grows up with close to no scarring. But that's not all." The enchantress licked her lips greedily. "By bringing her here, we have the opportunity to heal, not only her but the entire forest of Albadone. You see, enchanting isn't limited to runestones and ancient symbols. Enchanting is a blessing from the True One, and, with it, we can warp and shape nature itself. But every enchantment has a cost, for it is not our place to bend the natural world to our will."

The enchantress took a sip from her bowl of stew, then continued, "Some lower enchantments, like creating a purple runestone of *Life*, for example, have a very minimal cost—enchanted elements, natural ingredients, occasionally blood... Other higher runestones, like this one," she touched the yellow runestone at her neck, "can cost a life. Certain other enchantments have a cost that is more... symbolic than it is material—a woman apologizing to all the neighbors she's wronged or a father giving up his humanity to save a dying daughter, for example. Some costs may seem too extreme to most people. But I have a feeling you aren't most people." The woman paused as if expecting an answer. When it didn't come, she asked, "Are you willing to hear me out?"

Ashe set her bowl on the cave floor. She looked over at Sesha, at the gentle rising and falling of her breath as she snoozed. Then she turned to the enchantress and nodded, somewhat reluctantly.

"Albadone has been burned and scarred, much as you both have, because of the greed of a single man. This fool thought that he could bend nature to his will, but his methods exploited the Cycle of Nature, and as I've already said:

everything has a cost." The enchantress took a deep breath, her expression appeared pained. "It brings me no joy to tell you this, but the cost for your daughter's life and the life of the entire forest is... your daughter."

For a moment, Ashe wasn't sure if she had heard correctly. But, when she looked at the enchantress' face, it was clear that the woman had meant what she said. Ashe stood, shaking her head.

"I am very sorry," the enchantress apologized. "This is the cost. The will of the True One may seem unjust, but it is His will. Who are we to argue? This is the cost."

Ashe walked over to the cot, still shaking her head. She picked up Sesha. Mother Adriel stood, with unflinching calm. "A runestone of *Life* can only soothe. It cannot mend her broken flesh." The woman's voice felt lecturing, grave. "Surrender the girl to me, and she will be healed and live a long and healthy life. That is my guarantee to you. If you do not, she will no doubt succumb to her wounds within a week—or less. Are you willing to let your child die so that you may hold her until the time comes?" Tears dripped down Ashe's cheeks. Mother Adriel sighed, lowering her voice. "Being a mother means making difficult choices. I know that better than most. I've been a mother too, countless times before. In her heart, a mother always knows what's best for her children."

Ashe clung onto Sesha tightly, unwilling to let her go. What sort of monster would ask a mother to sacrifice her child? Ashe turned to leave, but some part of her knew the woman was right: there was no chance Sesha would live much longer without a healer to be found and with supplies growing scarce. What was she to do?

"Think about it," Mother Adriel said, her voice level. "If I wanted your child, I would have poisoned that stew and taken her from you. It would have been easy enough to do so, but it wouldn't have been a sacrifice—no cost would have been paid. If you don't do this, your child is as good as dead. Think about it, girl."

Ashe's tears fell onto Sesha's bandages. This wasn't what she had wanted—this cost was too high. She imagined leaving this awful woman and going away, anywhere but here. But to where? The woman said Sesha would live a long and happy life. Wouldn't she be a bad mother to deny her child that? Her hands shook—had she made up her mind? She kissed Sesha's forehead and then held her out to the enchantress.

"You're doing the right thing," the enchantress said, as she took the baby from Ashe's arms. "What's her name?"

"Sesha," Ashe managed to whisper between bitter sobs.

Mother Adriel lifted the baby in the air and said solemnly, "True One, this woman surrenders her child, Sesha, to You, so that You may right a wrong." Then the enchantress lowered the baby and turned to Ashe. "You must leave now. I have much work to do."

Ashe reached for her child to say one last goodbye, but the enchantress pulled the baby away. "This isn't your child anymore," Mother Adriel said coldly.

The words were a stab to Ashe's heart. It took everything inside of her to turn and leave. She headed down the winding mountain path as if stumbling through a dream. At the base of the mountain, the fog swallowed her once more as she walked through the woods, directionless, tears flowing freely from her eyes. Eventually, she lacked even the strength to cry anymore. Before she realized it, night had fallen. How long had she been walking? And in which direction? The sound of a babbling brook lulled her to sleep. When had she laid down? It didn't matter—nothing mattered now. She had surrendered her daughter. What sort of mother was she? No. No longer a mother at all—that was the cost. Elfred was taken from her. And she had given up their daughter. She had nothing left—nothing left to live for.

Morning came, and her mouth felt as if it were filled with sand. The previous night had been a blur of misery and sadness. Ashe tried as hard as she could to dispel any thoughts of her daughter. She found herself in what she imagined was a small clearing—it was hard to tell because of the thick fog that stained the surroundings. She stood to angry feet and made her way towards the rushing sounds of the river. The water was clear, in stark contrast to how the Chleo had been a few days earlier. She knelt over the river to drink: the water felt crisp and refreshing in her dry mouth and tasted almost sweet—the best she had ever had. She turned her face upstream: a doe and her fawn were bent over the river, drinking together.

Ashe crossed the cold river, this time with a bit more difficulty as the current now moved with more strength than it had the day before. She trudged forward in no particular direction. The sound of hoofs hitting a road and wooden wheels turning approached from several feet away.

She followed the sound until she reached the *Red Road*—the road that led from Vizen all the way to Rondhill in the south-east and then onward towards Sol Forne and the southern coast. *Rondhill!* A mule cart emerged from the fog and its driver nodded his head to her with a neighborly smile. Next to him sat a young girl of about six or seven, with light red hair. In the back of the cart were two women and a young child with a soot-covered face. The cart came to a halt a few feet away. The girl that sat next to the driver hopped down and skipped to Ashe with the sincerest look of joy she had seen in months.

"We're headed to Rondhill," the girl announced proudly. "He said you can join us if you're headed that way."

Ashe looked at the woodsfolk faces in the wagon. She thought of Alanda—had the woman already reached Rondhill? What would Alanda think of her when she found out what she had done to her child?

She turned to the girl's bright and expectant face and nodded. The child then took her by the hand and led her to the wagon. "I'm Ellie." *If the True One places a helper in your path, don't hesitate to follow.*

The women were polite enough. One was Elyma, the young mother of the soot-faced little boy, who explained that they had left Pevine after the riot to meet family in Rondhill. Her husband Ellio, the driver, had work waiting for him there. The other woman, Myr, Ellie's mother, smiled politely but didn't say much—her eyes were gray and distant. They had been lucky, Elyma said—*in more ways than you know*, Ashe thought while watching the woman clean her son's face with a bit of spit. Would she ever be able to touch her daughter again?

Suddenly, a thought flashed through her mind as she felt her pocket. The runestone of *Guidance* still sat inside. Yvan said it had only a couple more uses, if that. That would be enough.

One day, when Albadone had healed, that stone would guide her to Sesha. It was only a matter of time—and patience. But a mother would always wait. Yes. That's what she was and forever would be—a mother.

About The Authors

Élan Marché and Christopher Warman met in high school in Oklahoma in 2009. After dating for a decade, they got married in 2020. They currently live in Los Angeles where they work and spend their time watching TV, reading, writing, cooking delicious meals, and generally enjoying each other's company.

www.ingramcontent.com/pod-product-compliance
Lightning Source LLC
LaVergne TN
LVHW041806060526
838201LV00046B/1143